KIRBY, my dear chap, may I present Miss Christina Kelway? Miss Kelway, Lord Falkner."

The tall figure turned, "Miss Kelway, a pleasure." He raised his head from the modest bow and Chris found herself looking straight into the blue eyes she had first seen beside the Nile. "Sidi," she gasped.

The blue eyes held hers for one second ... then looked away. There was not a flash of recognition in them.

Fawcett Coventry Books
by Caroline Arnett:

CLARISSA   23930 $1.75

MELINDA   23477 $1.75

Buy them at your local bookstore or use this handy coupon for ordering.

This offer expires 1 June 80   8999

CHRISTINA

a novel by

Caroline Arnett

FAWCETT COVENTRY • NEW YORK

CHRISTINA

Published by Fawcett Coventry Books, a unit of CBS Publications,
the Consumer Publishing Division of CBS Inc.

ISBN: 0-449-50096-9

Printed in the United States of America

First Fawcett Coventry Printing: September 1980

10 9 8 7 6 5 4 3 2 1

In loving memory of
L.C.T. and T.A.T.
who did so much.

Chapter One

The moonlight had drawn all the golden color from the sand and left it a bleached white. The three palms that stood alone were tufted black bands stretching up toward the high bank, and the river beyond them lay, a shine of silver, broken briefly by a slow-moving, white-sailed felucca. No matter how often Christina stood thus, admiring, it seemed more beautiful each time. She would miss it all, even the hateful sand, when they went home to England. She turned her back on the Nile and plowed, for she always thought of walking in sand as plowing, toward her own special tomb. It was small, well back from the edge of the bank, against a low cliff, and hidden by two high, nearly overlapping sand dunes. Her father had scorned it as unimportant, so she had made it her own, where she could come and do her own drawings and paintings and a goal for her evening stroll.

As she rounded the ends of the two dunes into the space before the two pillars, she lifted her eyes, for the moonlight would be penetrating through the narrow porch. Often when she came she could see how the wind had shifted the sand both outside and within. She wished again she had been able to persuade her father to have the place cleared just a little but he had held it was merely a waste of his time and that of the few workmen he had hired. Of course there was no knowing for whom the tomb had been made, but Christina was sure it was a beloved daughter of an important man, for on one wall where the sand had not mounted more than three feet a girl was shown playing a harp in a boat. Christina had named her Clio and thought of the small tomb as belonging to them both. She picked up her feet—the heavy shoes her father had insisted she wear on account of the occasional snake were clumsy—and looked ahead again. And stopped. A black blob of a vulture sat above the square portal and at the foot of one of the lotus-topped pillars was a heap that was not sand. Who could have come to *her* tomb? Walking in sand made no sound. She moved around the space and approached the heap from the side. It was a man sitting with his head on his knees. He was wearing the coarse white cotton shirt and short trousers of the fellaheen, but they were torn and dirty. His hair was white, his skin dark, and ribs showed through a rent in the shirt. As her shadow fell on him he tried to lift his head and dropped it. "Water," he croaked. "Water."

She half turned away, deciding not to disturb this exhausted wanderer, and then realized he had spoken in English, slurred but quite clear. Any traveler was helped when in need, and without asking questions. If this man needed water she should bring him some. It was not far back to the storehouse where they lived. She leaned down. "I am going for water," she said slowly, and did not wait to see if he made any sign of having understood.

At the storehouse, to the left of the large tomb, her father was at work in the front room he called his studio. Two lamps on the plank table lighted the paper before him from which he was so carefully transferring and enlarging his sketches. No matter how deep he was in a problem he always knew her step on the stone floor. "Chris," he called. "Is all well?"

For once she wasn't quite sure, but she reassured him as she crossed to the opposite storeroom which they used for dining and to hold supplies. As was the custom, they had brought utensils and lamps with them, along with mattresses and linen, and had bought a number of the local earthenware jugs, whose evaporation kept the Nile water cool and clear. She took one, found a woven basket, and added a cotton napkin and a section of bread and went slowly back to the little tomb. The man was still as she had left him. As he felt her by him he croaked again "Water," and raised his head.

She placed everything on the sand, poured a little water into a mug, and dipping in a corner of the napkin gently wiped the cracked, blackened lips. There came a long sigh. Five times she patted his mouth with the moistened cloth and then tipped in a little water. There was a pause and she tipped in more. She knew anyone so parched must take water slowly, so she sat back and waited and poured a little more. The moon had moved and now they were almost in shadow. But she knew the sun would beat on this spot for much of the day. He must move. She rose and tugged at his arm, but he sat motionless, head again on his hands.

After a few moments she spoke close to his ear. "You must move into the tomb . . . because of the sun . . . and the vultures will take your bread."

He waited a moment, as though gathering strength, then gave a croak. "Will crawl."

She moved everything out of his way. "Come," she said, and moved to the entrance. She knew just where

9

he could stay, out of the sun and out of sight. She looked back. The figure was crawling on knees and forearms, head sagging. It heaved itself over the low step and collapsed. He had to come farther. She took off her head scarf and thrust one end in his hand and gave a tug. Painfully he followed her around the bank of sand that half filled the right portion of the tomb and down to the wall at the end. There she shook his shoulder and tried to turn him. "You must sit up so you can drink."

When she returned he was sagging against the wall but opened his mouth when she poured a few drops on his face. She couldn't stay longer, and crouched down beside him. "I must go," she began, removing her scarf from his clutch.

One bony hand moved and clutched her robe. "No," he mumbled. "Don't let them get me."

"I won't," she promised. "Listen. I am leaving a jug of water and a mug and some bread beside you. When you can, break bits of bread in the mug, put in some water, and swallow when it is soft. I'll be back tomorrow with more water and food. Stay here. You are safe."

Outside she brushed at the marks in the sand with the bottom of her robe. Sand never held clear imprints but it could show indentations that might be revealing. Then she was walking quickly. She was halfway back to the storehouse when she heard horses trotting along the bank, and moved faster.

The horses reached her when she was almost there, so she stopped and faced them. The man in the lead raised his hand and the men behind him came to a halt. He swung down from his horse and came toward her. The moon was low but she could see that he wore a uniform and had dark hair and moustache.

"Pardon me, mademoiselle." He swept off his cap and bowed. "I trust we did not frighten you." His English had a slight French accent.

"Why, no," she said coolly. "Have you come to see my father?"

"Ah, I have come where I intended. You must be the daughter of Lord Ingram. Allow me to introduce myself, Captain Oudenard of the Patrol Troops of Pasha Mohammed Ali."

Deciding no extra courtesy was called for, Christina inclined her head and murmured his name.

"I am surprised to see you out alone in the evening, mademoiselle," he said in a strange tone.

"No one ever comes here. I often take a stroll before retiring." She hoped her voice implied it was none of his affair.

"Then you may be able to help me. We are seeking an escaped slave, one who fled a week or so ago from a sherif near Darau."

"But that is far up the Nile," she exclaimed, "nearly to Aswan. And a slave?"

"Or a servant, or a prisoner, that was not too clear," he said easily. "But apparently valuable. The sherif is furious and begged assistance from his friend of Luxor. I am there briefly, and was asked to assist. We are always instructed to win the goodwill of these local chiefs."

"But no one could have come this far alone, walking, for so many days." Her tone was thoughtful. "He has probably drowned."

"My thought exactly, Miss Ingram," he agreed cheerfully.

"Miss Kelway," she corrected absently. "You must come and ask my father. He will not care for the interruption but it is time he stopped working." They were safely distant from her tomb and would hardly go back that way since there was a road along the river. She turned toward the glow from the storehouse, and the captain walked beside her.

"You do not object to living in this—this primitive fashion?" he asked a little hesitantly.

"Why, no. It is interesting. We have a servant who comes every day with fresh food and does the cooking. We are quite comfortable. We English are accustomed to strange modes of living, you know, when doing explorations of any kind in foreign lands."

At the entrance to the storehouse she called, "Father," and led the captain inside to the left. "We have a visitor."

Her father looked up and frowned. "At this time of night?" He rose from the table, the lamplight lengthening his shadow on the wall behind him.

"This is Captain Oudenard, searching for an escaped slave of some sherif up near Aswan."

The captain stepped forward and bowed. "At your service, sir. But I must ask if you have seen any fleeing man."

"Certainly not. No one comes here but our own servant. A slave? Disgraceful. I hear they are treated badly. I am surprised an officer lends himself to pursuing one."

Christina looked at her father proudly. He was such a tall, handsome man in spite of his beard, for which she could feel no affection, though she knew it added to his consequence here in Egypt. He amusedly allowed her to trim it with her scissors. His hazel eyes were so lively and so often laughing she was very pleased when someone told her hers were like his. She came back from her fond survey to hear the captain saying defensively, "I am only following my orders, sir. We must keep in with these local chiefs."

"I am surprised the Pasha in Cairo takes the trouble, but then you said you were on patrol, so he must have some concern for the petty beys and sherifs in addition to sending his tax gatherers. No, sir, I have not seen whomever it is you seek." He bent his head slightly and the captain bowed and practically backed away to his horse and the line of men.

Christina waited until the sound of hooves faded to the north. "I hope he doesn't come again."

"That's not likely," her father said comfortably. "Shocking business. Glad I haven't seen the poor devil, for I'd have had to say so. We must keep in with the local chiefs too, you know, and the presents I gave them won't buy friendly relations for long. Well, I was about to stop anyway. You're turning in? We'll start work early tomorrow. We have so little time left . . . Sleep well, my dear."

Chris took a lantern, and wished for the hundredth time it was a better one, kissed her father's cheek, and walked to the back storeroom on the right. Bringing their own bedding and utensils with them had certainly added to their comfort, she reflected, though with no way to drive pegs in the granite blocks of the walls, she was a little tired of living out of her boxes and the chest her father had had made for her. Since the storehouse, for her father was sure it had been built as such for the tomb nearby, had been empty since it was robbed many hundreds of years ago, no one came near to disturb them.

Sitting on the cot she began to brush her hair as she planned. She would have to go well before breakfast with food and water for the man. He must be the escaped slave the captain was chasing. And he was English. All the more reason to help him. Of course he would live since he had already survived so much. She would leave soon after dawn. She wished she could tell her father, but with his sense of duty she could not as long as there was any danger of that captain coming back to ask more questions. But she was sure she could manage for a while.

Above the line of bare hills across the river the sky was lightening to a pale gray as she set out. The basket did not feel heavy nor did she think of walking through the sand as plodding. This was the most interesting thing that had happened in their three months at the tomb, though she quickly rebuked herself, for of course the copying of the pictures on the walls was very interesting and important. How nice it would be to have someone new to talk to, when the man could talk again.

He was lying on his back and seemed asleep. She wished the light was not so dim here inside Clio's tomb. Light in Egypt was either too bright and hot or too dim, she had found. She could see he was long and very brown but the palms of the outflung hands were white. His face was all high cheekbones, forehead, nose, and chin, but it was not old in spite of the white hair. She touched his arm and he stirred and drew himself together.

"It's all right," she soothed. "It's me. I've brought some more water and bread and some chicken broth that I think is still all right though we had it for supper yesterday."

He was staring at her. "You. Last night," he croaked.

"Yes." She put down the basket. "All the water and bread are gone, I see. Do try to sit up so you can take some more."

He pushed himself up and then back to the wall, very slowly, and in a moment lifted his head partway. "Good of you," he gasped.

"Not at all," she told him briskly. "I couldn't let an Englishman be taken. Did you escape from a sherif or something up near Darau?"

He was as if frozen. "How—know?"

"A captain came by, said he was looking for an escaped slave. He went away when my father said he knew nothing about one. Don't worry, he won't come back, or if he does he won't come here, I promise. You must eat and rest." She put the jug and bowl and bread near his hand. Perhaps if she told him familiar things he would be reassured. "Here is the water." She lifted his hand and put it on the jug. "It is one of those earthenware jugs whose outside stays moist and keeps the water cool." The hand tightened on the handle. "Take it slowly. The bread is that flat dhourra that gets hard, so break it in pieces and put it in the soup. Here." She broke off a few pieces into the bowl. "I have to go. I can't come back until it is dark. I promise I will then." She was sorry to leave him, he looked so exhausted. But he wouldn't die, she told herself again, and putting the empty jug in her basket she went away.

For once she hardly noticed how her feet sank in the sand and had to be lifted from each indentation. She would have to find ways to do more for the man. She must find a name for him. He needed some utensils of his own, clothes to replace the torn and dirty shirt and trousers, more food. How long would it take him to recover some strength? There must be muscles along all those bones and he looked as if he had been quite strong. A glance to her right showed the river was turning to red gold. At the storehouse Ali was carrying the waterskin down the bank for the first of the day's supply. She was in time to restore basket and jug and be waiting at the table for her father, and, on Ali's return with the full skin, praise him for the two chickens he had brought along with melons and lentils and bread and cheese.

"We'll start on the second rooms," her father began eagerly. "We have all we can see of the first set. The

15

second shows our hero at his home, with his pleasures and sports, you remember. The open roof will be a great help, so we'll start wherever the light falls and follow it. Our Richard really led a most agreeable life."

"I wish we had another name for him." Christina was repeating herself. "Something that sounds more Egyptian than Richard."

"But we don't know their names," her father pointed out patiently. "Would you prefer Memphis or Karnak?"

That made her laugh. "No. I just like names for people and he seems such a nice man."

"Females always do like names for everything," he observed, "a touching trait, at times. I believe they feel if a thing or a person is named it is somehow made more real, even possessed, perhaps. I agree Richard is not appropriate, but it reminds me of my dear brother, who would undoubtedly have enjoyed all this with us. I wish, with you, we could read all the writings, the cartouches, know whom we are trying to preserve. But we must remember we are helping someone who will be deciphering the writings someday."

With her box of watercolors and brushes and pad she followed him from the storehouse across the hundred yards of sand to the tomb, carved into the face of the low cliff, and around the piles of stone that had once hidden the entrance. It was not a large tomb, like the few they had seen, but great care had gone into the carvings on the two round pillars that flanked the open door and those on the walls of the shallow portico which could be seen above the undulating piles of sand that reached halfway to the painted ceiling. The sand from the hall had been carried away, but there was neither time nor money to hire more workers to clear the whole tomb, even though the foreman from the Pasha in Cairo had given permission to clear the place and ordered all to assist the Lord Ingram. The colored carvings that

16

could be seen in the first two rooms had been copied, so they halted at the entrance of the second set. The open hall continued to the blackness of the last room where once the sarcophagus had lain but which now was nearly filled with drifts of sand.

"We will start with the wall on the left of the left room and move around it and hope we will have time to complete both rooms before we leave," Lord Ingram directed happily. "We must thank again whoever thought to leave off the roof of the hall."

"Indeed yes. And these pictures are more fun, for the people are enjoying boating and dancing girls and feasts and hunting. I had forgotten the borders are full of animals and flowers. They are like the ones in the little tomb."

"Indeed? I confess these walls will be easier to transfer than the battles and processions," her father said absently and started up the sand bank by the first pillar. Planting his feet as firmly as possible in the sliding sand he surveyed the first long panel. "Not so spirited as when he is driving his war chariot, but very agreeable."

By using the first pillar Chris came up beside him. The personage, Richard, was sitting in a barge that was being poled by four men while two more sat in the bow, one with a small harp and the other holding a flute to his lips. Facing the handsome man sat a lady, slightly smaller in scale, with a fan. The two were smiling at each other, ignoring the heads of crocodiles that protruded from the wavy water at their side.

"They look so happy," Chris said a little wistfully. "If only we could read all those signs ... and the paintings are so bright." She opened her box to make notes and samples of the colors as her father began to copy the figures and hieroglyphics. Balancing her small paintbox and pad was awkward and when the jug of

17

water tipped a little she stopped to rest. It all took so long and she had to be so exact about every detail. "Father," she burst out, "is this really worth all our time and trouble? Is anyone in England going to be interested in anything out of Egypt?"

"Oh, yes, my dear. I told you the Prince of Wales is having lotus-flower capitals put on the pillars that support the roof of the kitchen at the palace he is building at Brighton. They will excite interest. And Freddy Lethbridge talked of the growing popularity of Egyptian-style furniture."

"But it will take the scholars years to make out what is on that stone the French found at Rosetta."

"True; and lucky we are to have obtained it. But they are working away and with the writings in three scripts they'll be able to decipher these hieroglyphics. That will excite everyone. And when that happens it will be of great assistance to have clear copies on paper to work on instead of having to go and peer at statues and slabs of stone taken from no one knows where."

"All they will do is say thank you to you and have no idea of the work we have done."

"Quite true." He was cheerful about it. "But you and I will have the satisfaction of having helped open a new world. And I promise you again that when we return to England I will see to it that you have a gay season in London to make up for these months when you have been so patient and helpful."

"Oh, Father, you know I delight in being with you. I don't need a reward. But I confess," she added a little wistfully, "it will be nice not to have to live in sand and to wear a dress and have my hair clean."

At that he chuckled. "You always look charming, in spite of the sand and that enveloping galabia you were instructed to wear at all times. And we'll be leaving soon." He began to draw again.

Christina subsided and became absorbed in trying to match the shade of red on the face of Richard and the female before him and wished the ancient people had had a color in their palate that would correspond to flesh tones and had not had to make everyone look like a Red Indian. She was surprised when Ali came to tell them lunch was ready.

That brought her back to her problem. "I am going to Luxor this afternoon," she announced over a dish of lentils and onions and dates. "We are tired of chicken and I will get some mutton and eggs and more fruit and vegetables. I'll walk with Ali to the village and hire those two asses we use."

"Good, my dear. Get anything you wish." Suddenly he smiled, his face lighting with affection. "I must say again I am glad you are with me. It would be dreary work without you. Remember to keep your hood partly across your face."

She rose and kissed him. "I'm glad I'm here, too." And went to tell Ali of the expedition.

The village, a half mile to the south on the road beside the river, was hardly large enough for that name. Here the band of green that lined the Nile on both sides was narrow because of cliffs. Beneath some palms crouched ten windowless huts of mud bricks with garden plats on either side. Chickens wandered, pigeons filled the air with wings and coos, and the patient water buffalo, who looked so fierce and was so gentle, trod round and round to raise the waterwheel. Ali's brother had two asses for rent. Chris enjoyed the ride, for the road was busy and there was much to see, and when two camels went by she nearly clapped, for they were not common here.

Christina had learned a little Arabic and Ali, a cheerful, obedient man, a few words of English so they could communicate and laugh when they couldn't. The asses were left with a cousin of Ali's and they went on foot to the souk. Two baskets and food were the first purchases. Then, telling Ali to wait, and thankful he had long lost his curiosity about the ways of foreigners, she took one basket and turned down a narrow alley that wound between shops where clothes festooned the entrances and tables held household wares. Purchasing anything was a slow process but at last she was finished and rejoined Ali and then the asses for a leisurely ride back. At supper that night they had mutton roasted over charcoal with onions and Lord Ingram was so pleased he forgot to mourn the lack of beef in Egypt. Over the fruit he said he would heartily approve another expedition at any time, which made her wish she had gone more often in the past.

Chapter Two

When Ali had carried everything down the bank to the river for washing and returned and departed, and her father was settled at his table, Christina filled a basket with what she could carry and started for Clio's tomb. It was already dark, for the twilights were very short, but there were stars, and their reflections on the water seemed to add light to the air. The stars were so much brighter here than in England they seemed nearer and larger and some evenings she just sat and watched them for a while. Now as she tramped she was wondering if she had brought enough food.

At the tomb entrance she gasped, for a part of the shadow moved slowly toward her. "You—frightened me," she managed and waited as he took another step.

"Forgive me." The words came more clearly. "Wished to show you better."

Warmly she assured him she could see that and was pleased, though she could also see he was wavering a little. "Let us sit on the step and I'll show you what I have brought." Something told her not to reach out a hand to help him turn and pace the three steps. Sitting down quickly she pretended not to notice the relief with which he lowered himself and leaned against the pillar.

"Water. Always cool. Delicious," he brought out painfully.

"Isn't it," she agreed as she busied herself with the basket. "Father says the Nile water is held the best in the world. Here," she waved a hand, "I am putting out what I brought, another spoon, knife, fork, a jug of soup made of onions and lentils, and some lamb cut in very small bits, and of course water. Be sure to carry it all inside before it is light." A well-brought-up girl would not acknowledge she knew that men wore trousers, but this was no time to be ignorant. "Also, here is a pair of trousers, the largest I could find, sandals, and a shirt, all just what the fellaheen wear, as you know. What you have on are too ragged and dirty for any comfort. Tomorrow morning I will bring bananas and eggs and water. I hope," she added a little anxiously, "that the soup will put more strength in you."

He straightened a little. "It will. Very grateful." He paused. "To whom do I owe—this—this bounty?"

"I am Christina Kelway. What is your name?"

He gave a sigh. "Forgotten. Been called Sidi so long . . ."

"Don't worry. That will do for now." It was a comfort to have a name to use in one's mind.

"You're English," he began laboriously, turning his head toward her. "Heard a mad Englishman by the Nile. Am looking for him."

She laughed. "That must be my father. All think he is mad because he does not look for antiquities as foreigners usually do. He says it is a protection. He'll help you."

"Must get stronger." Determination lay under the words.

"But I do not understand," and she frowned, "why

you were almost dying of thirst when there was the Nile below the bank. You could have gone down to it for water."

"Afraid," he said simply. "Almost caught one night. Seen by a boat. Hid. Day...too many people. Found little food. Afraid fall...be found...sent back." He sighed again and his head went back against the pillar.

She could understand all that. If the place he had been was so dreadful he had had to escape he'd run no risk of being captured no matter how famished and thirst-ridden he had become. "How lucky you spoke in English," she said impulsively.

"What came to mind. Now seems natural."

Somehow that seemed to her a good sign. She rose and picked up the basket. "I must go. Do remember to move everything inside. No one comes here, but some child might wander around. Eat everything slowly. I'll be back. Good night."

He raised his head. "Forgive not rising," he said quite clearly. As she turned she saw his head drop forward again.

He was certainly stronger in every way, she told herself with some pride as she strolled back. As she paused to look at the river beyond the belt of green she heard hoofbeats and began to hurry.

Again the horseman caught up with her just before she reached the storehouse. Captain Oudenard swung down beside her. "Ah. I am as fortunate as I had hoped. Again I find Miss Kelway alone and strolling."

"Good evening," she said coolly and had to stop because he was standing in front of her. "Are you still pursuing the escaped slave?"

"No longer. I waited for an extra day to see if word was brought in, but there was none. So I decided I deserved the reward of another visit with you. You

23

must be lonely here. Or are you on your way to an assignation?"

"With a crocodile? You know there are no foreigners in the neighborhood." She showed her amusement. "And, no, sir, I am never lonely here."

"Now you have a visitor. Me."

"How kind of you to come to call. You wish to see my father?" She stepped to the left and around him casually.

"Not at all. I am come to enjoy the evening with you," and an arm went around her shoulder.

She shook it off and faced him. "Captain. You forget yourself." She put a haughty note in her voice.

"Not at all," he laughed. "I believe you would enjoy a little dalliance, as would any attractive girl."

"I do not dally with anyone. You are no gentleman if you would attempt to force your attentions on me."

"Though you are a cold English girl you would soon enjoy them." He seized her right arm and forced her to face him. "I will show you."

"Let go, or I will scream and bring my father with his gun. He is a very good shot. He disposes of vultures and kites and jackals that come too near. He would not hesitate to shoot you if you molest me, I assure you."

"You are trying to frighten me. Come now . . ."

"I am sparing your life by not screaming," she told him as icily and firmly as she could. "Now, go." She wrenched her arm from his hand and wished it were more light so she could freeze him more effectively.

His hand dropped. "I do not believe you. I could have you on my horse in a minute."

"Not before I scream and my father comes."

He shrugged. "Very well, Miss Kelway. I was hoping to find some way of persuading you to tell me where the gold and jewels are hidden. There are many ways to make a girl talk. But now I merely ask you."

"Gold and jewels?" She was so astonished she forgot her hauteur. "We have no gold and jewels."

"Do not so pretend. Your father descended into the pit of the tomb and brought up a cask full of gold and jewels. It is hidden here, somewhere, until you can carry it to England. Better you should share it with me than with some bey or sherif who would take it all."

She was glad she could actually laugh. "Someone has been telling you fairy tales. You should have learned you cannot believe the natives. This tomb is empty of everything but sand, as it was when we came here. My father did go down into the pit below the hall with the help of three fellaheen from the village. Two went down with him. They found nothing, not even the sarcophagus! The men told that to everyone, and all believed them, and no one has come back."

"That is not what I heard," he said sullenly. "It is known the English are clever at deceiving. He could have hidden it, gone back for it later."

"With two men watching him the whole time? Even the bey has believed there is nothing. You have lost your senses as well as your manners. Since you have failed in everything, good night, Captain Oudenard." Determinedly but with a little trepidation she turned her back on him and headed for the storehouse. As she restored the basket and jug to their places she hoped the captain had not noticed her left hand. Now he was gone, for she could hear a horse cantering southward, she found she was shaking a little, but she was proud of the coolness she had maintained and the set-down she had given him. To go to bed now would be too dull, so she went down to the river for a swim and to wash her hair so it would look better for a day or so.

At Clio's tomb Sidi was leaning against the pillar at the entrance. As she neared he took several steps and reached for the basket. "Good morning," he said formally, and then with a smile that lighted his bony face, "You see I am better today than yesterday." He spoke slowly but with more assurance. "I can walk for a little."

"Splendid." She sat down on the step. "But I must warn you that Captain Oudenard came by last night, for he said he had remained in Luxor in case any word came of you. None has, but when it is truly light do stay hidden."

"Then I will walk inside," he agreed.

"You must be careful there, too, though I have seen no snakes here. And do not go back where it is dark or attempt to reach the far end of the hall. There is an open pit in the way."

"Open pit?"

"Yes." She moved to point down the hall. "Perhaps you do not know. There is in all tombs." She hesitated, wondering what he did know but deciding to tell him anyway. "The cell at the very end of the hall just held a mummy case, a handsome one but empty. The mummy itself, in another case, was placed in a pit below the paving to hide it from tomb robbers. They always found it, though, and always took away everything, even the mummies and the cases, and did not bother to replace the slab they had pried up. This pit is not deep, only ten feet or so. My father, to please me, went down to look and reported everything was gone, as it was in the tomb where he is working." She felt he was looking at her and turned and found he was studying her from under lowered lids.

"You are young." Surprise filled his voice. "I had not seen clearly. And so kind."

She looked at him. The face was still all bones under the tight skin, beneath the white hair. Again, the face and the hair did not match. "I think you are also," she said as slowly, "though it is hard to be sure with your hair."

"Hair?" He put up one hand and touched it. "Blond?"

"It's white, you know." She pushed back her hood and gave her head a shake to show what she meant. "It probably got bleached in the sun," which should be a comforting thought. "It will grow in properly, I'm sure. You better take a piece of that old shirt and make a turban. Where are your new clothes?"

"Inside, until I can go for a swim."

"Be careful and go very early. There are paths through the bushes, you can hide if you have to." The sand around them was gathering color from the brightening sky. "I must go."

He rose with her. "Will be saying every day, thank you . . ."

"There's no need, you have quite often enough." She made her words matter-of-fact, for he was still a pitiful figure, in such contrast to his good manners. "Here is your breakfast and luncheon. I'll be back tonight."

"Too much trouble for you," he protested.

"But I am glad to, and to see you improving every day." She nodded and went toward the piles of sand. In fact, she should be grateful to him for bringing her something so interesting to help fill the evenings, when she could not paint because the light of the lamps changed the values of the colors and yet was too dim for pleasurable reading.

The next two days were tranquil, even the brief morning and evening visits to Clio's tomb and a steadily strengthening Sidi. One of the afternoons, when there was nothing for her to color for her father, she took her paints and paper to her own pictures. Sidi was asleep in the darkest corner. She decided, regretfully, he needed sleep more than her company, but she drew and painted happily for a while and left him still asleep.

27

The third morning he was standing at the entrance and wearing his new shirt and trousers and a pleased look on his gaunt face. "Good morning, Miss Kelway. You see a new man." He spoke more quickly, with such pleasure. "Last night, when the moon was up, I found my way to the river. I soaked in it until almost dawn. I climbed the bank very slowly, I confess. But I have not felt so well in what I believe to be a long time."

"Congratulations." She laughed, sharing his pleasure. "You do look much better." He was different, as though his hours in the Nile had refreshed and restored him. "We must soon think what to do next."

He was facing the growing light. His eyes widened at her words and for the first time she saw them clearly and that they were an intense blue. "Oh, dear," she exclaimed in dismay.

"What is wrong?" he asked anxiously.

"Your eyes. They are so very blue. Not at all the thing for this country."

"Are they?" He was not interested. "I did not know. Is that so very bad?"

"Yes, I fear. They do not go with the name Sidi. Though there are many different shades of eyes here in Egypt. I have noticed blue and all shades of gray and brown. It is because the Vandals came the whole way across northern Africa in the fifth century, my father says, and the Greeks came south for trade. But I have seen none like yours. But you seldom open them widely, so perhaps the color will not be noticed. And now I think of it your beard is not scraggly enough for an Egyptian."

He put one hand to his chin. "But I have no razor."

"It wouldn't do for you to be clean-shaven," she pointed out seriously. "Your skin would be white and definitely peculiar."

"Yes. What can be done?"

"I can hack at it with my scissors, make it look more like those I see in the streets. But no need to fret ourselves about it now." She watched him proudly as he walked into the tomb for the empty jugs. He moved and spoke easily now. That was her achievement. She had brought him back to life and all by herself. Never before had she accomplished anything so important and gratifying.

The next morning he took the basket from her quickly, brushing aside her regrets that the food, like their own, was so sadly monotonous, and seized her hand. "Come. I have something to show you."

He led her around the edge of the pile of sand in the hall and toward the back of the tomb. Part of the roof had been removed or fallen and they skirted the block of stone to the space where she had been just once, with her father. Sand was heaped irregularly and just beyond yawned the pit. At the side of a heap of sand Sidi halted. "Perhaps I should not show you. It will not be pleasant for a young lady."

"I have seen many peculiar and sometimes upleasant sights since coming to Egypt," she pointed out gaily. "I am sure I will not faint, no matter what."

"Pray do not, for if you should I would have no idea how to go about reviving you. Here, then..." He stepped to beside the sand and, kneeling down, began to lift some away with both hands. In a moment what looked like a black stick was uncovered.

She knelt beside him. "What is it?"

"It is an arm, without any hand, as you see. There is more." He brushed away at the pile, and what might have been but wasn't a pile of sticks emerged. "I think it is one of the original tomb robbers," he went on eagerly. "I have heard of such, and that all the tombs are empty and have been for many centuries. This one must have had a falling-out with his companions. Else why

29

should the hand be gone? And, don't look, but the back of the skull over there is quite crushed in."

There was nothing in the black sticks to disgust, Chris told herself, and it was remarkable to see bones that were so very old. "Interesting," she said steadily. "I am sure you are right."

The blue eyes gave her a wide look of approval. "I knew you would not be missish. But there is more." Gently he turned over the blackened bones that could hardly be regarded as legs or ribs and pointed to what lay beneath. Fingers lay on top of something round. "They took what was in one hand, you see, but he probably fell on this one. I waited to see what he is holding until you came, for this tomb is yours by right of discovery. Shall we find out?"

"Of course. Please." She hoped it would be nothing worse than bones.

He slid out the black object. It might once have been of leather, but it fell apart as he drew it to them and they were looking at a pile of gold. With one finger he stirred the pile and it became a heap of small figurines. Animals. On one side lay a donkey, an owl beside him, a lotus flower next. "I'll be damned..." he murmured, and stirred the pile again. "There are a dozen at least, beautifully done."

"Oooooh," breathed Chris. "They're so delicate..."

"There's more." He moved the figures to one side. Underneath lay a necklace, gold, turquoise, and carnelian, tangled with two earrings and a brooch.

"I was right," Chris said wonderingly. "This was a tomb of a lady. Oh, it is *lovely*."

"We will take them to my room. Can you carry them in your robe?" She held out her skirt for the pile. "I'll just cover this chap up again." With two sweeps of his hand he had sand sliding down from the pile and covering the black bones. As Christina reached the entrance she saw the sun must be up.

She nearly dropped the corners of her robe. "I am so late," she gasped.

"A few minutes more won't matter then," he said over her shoulder. "Do sit down and let us look."

On the doorstep she spread out the cloth and the shining gold. There were fourteen figures, each done with a delicate perfection. "Even that horrid crocodile has teeth," she exclaimed with awe, "and they all have eyes, claws, ears. Oh, they are beautiful!" The necklace was of narrow gold wire with a series of pendants alternating turquoise and carnelian beads and a turquoise flower at the center. Unable to resist, she pushed back the top of the enveloping robe, lifted the necklace, and clasped it around her neck. "I wish I had a mirror," she sighed as she took it off.

"You will have a mirror when you wear it for some occasion," he said lightly. "It looks a little tight but can be spread."

She looked at the sky. "Oh, I am so late."

"Why does it matter?" He was handing her the basket.

"Father would be concerned if I did not join him at breakfast, go to look for me. Ali would wonder why I should take a walk carrying a basket."

"Ali?"

"Our servant, from the village. He is cheerful but stupid. All the working people are stupid, and very curious. Good-by."

Her thoughts moved more quickly than her feet. Would she show the treasure trove to her father? She should. There was no law in Egypt against carrying away statues, anything found in the country, though she had heard local chiefs usually had to be bribed. There were no private owners of these barren cliffs and sands. But her father was so strictly honorable. He might feel it should all be given to that Pasha who ruled for the Turks in Cairo. And he was so generous. He might make a present of any animal to any friend. She could not bear that. They had belonged to Clio and now they were hers, and, perhaps, Sidi's, she acknowledged. She *must* hide them. Officials, soldiers, servants thought nothing of rummaging in boxes and chests and you had to stand by and smile. She must think of something. And there was Sidi. Surely he was strong enough now to walk to the storehouse.

Her father was coming from his studio as she left her room and smiling at her with such affection that for a moment she almost changed her mind about her treasures. But common sense told her to hold to her resolve. But suddenly she decided she would bring Sidi that very night to her father.

Chapter Three

So the next evening, after Sidi had finished the supper Chris had brought him, while she played with the golden animals, he walked back to the storehouse with her. They went slowly, for he insisted on carrying the basket. Tucked down below the jugs and bowl was the gold, wrapped in a piece of the old shirt. As they walked she said she would hide it in her chest and he suggested he make a false bottom, if wood could be obtained, to keep it from any prying fingers. And she talked a little of her father and his interests and travels to distract the man beside her, for he plodded slowly. At the storehouse she told him to lean against the wall and wait while she put everything away and lingered a little to give him time to recover his breath, for the walk had obviously tired him. When she returned she picked up his hand and led him to the studio.

"Father," she began, and could not keep the excitement from her voice, "pray halt your work for a moment. I have a new friend to introduce. He is in need of help and you will know what to do."

Lord Ingram rose. "A new friend? In need of help?"

"May I present Sidi, who is in mortal danger from

that French captain." Once her father's sympathies were engaged all would be well.

"Any friend of my daughter is most welcome." Lord Ingram walked to the end of the table and held out his hand. Chris dropped the thin fingers she was holding and Sidi advanced and took it. "Let us make ourselves as comfortable as possible." He nodded. "The stools are hard but one becomes accustomed to them."

Chris shoved one against the pillar and gave Sidi a little push toward it so he could lean back and pushed another beside it.

"Now." Her father returned to his own and surveyed them both. "Christina, you seem in charge at the moment. Perhaps you can tell me how—Sidi—has come to see us."

"I found him, Father, one night, sitting by the little tomb. He asked for water; he hadn't the strength to move. I took him a jug and for several days I have been carrying food and water to him until he could walk enough to come here." She glanced to her side and saw he was leaning back, eyes closed. "He is exhausted. Water. I should have thought." She hurried for a jug and a full mug which he took with a slightly shaking hand and drank slowly.

"Sorry, sir," he said clearly, and leaned back again.

Her father's look of astonishment was almost comical and he smiled. "I see you have learned it is best to obey the ladies in matters of importance. Do you feel you can tell us how you came to be here? Something has evidently been a nearly dire experience for you. Would you tell me your name and who you are?"

Sidi moved his head from side to side. "I can't, sir. I don't remember."

"What? That is incredible, man."

Again the head, wrapped in the awkward ragged

turban, moved in denial. "All I know is that for many months I have been called Sidi."

"You present us with an interesting mystery then." Lord Ingram propped one elbow on the table and rested his chin on his hand, brushing away a moth with the other. "What do you remember?"

Sidi took another sip. "I recall sitting in what may have been a tent. There was food before me and a pile of gold. There were figures sitting around and a man opposite me. I was laughing. Something crashed on my head." He paused and passed his hand across his face. "When I came to I was—was shackled and learned I was a slave of a sherif who called himself Ibn-El-Hahir. I could not work for a while. Always dizzy. Annoyed him and his men. Was beaten. Tried to protest. Was laughed at. Could not make myself understood." His voice was trailing away.

"Enough." Lord Ingram was off his stool and helping Sidi to his feet. "We'll talk more tomorrow. Would you object to sleeping in the tomb, my boy?"

"I would feel at home, sir." There was a hint of humor in the hoarse voice.

"I'm taking you there. Chris, hand me the water, please."

She started to follow with a lantern but decided there was enough light and they were better left alone, and so waited, with a little trepidation, for her father's return.

"Of course you did right," he told her approvingly, answering her unspoken question. "In fact, you did very well. I am proud of you. It is evident he is a gentleman born, no matter what brought him to this pass. I find I believe him, but I look forward to learning more tomorrow."

He told Ali the next morning before breakfast of the arrival of a friend who had been robbed and beaten and made his way with great difficulty to the tomb. It was done with such calm authority that no questions could be asked, even by a curious Arab. And Sidi stopped and spoke and Ali smiled and bowed.

"You know something of the language, then," Lord Ingram observed as they sat down. Chris had joined them.

"I had to, fast, sir. My vocabulary is limited, I know, and the accent probably atrocious."

"I learned some when I was here years ago and it returned, which is fortunate. Christina has learned a little. I do not find it, at least as spoken here, an attractive language." He reached for a banana. "Do you feel up to telling us more? I am most interested in your account."

"We can take our stools and sit outside by the wall," Chris broke in eagerly. "The sun is not high enough to give us a good light." Sidi was looking much better this morning, more alert, and his voice was coming smoothly. He must be relieved to be with friends. And it was important for her father to be assured and concerned.

When they were settled as comfortably as possible she asked quickly, "How long were you with that horrid sherif?"

"I have no way of judging time, but I was there for two floodings of the Nile, which I gather comes once a year." He was still speaking slowly, choosing his words, but with greater ease.

"What happened next, when you found where you were?"

"When I could work I was put to caring for the few horses and asses. Next I was sent into the fields but I did not work hard enough. Then the sherif seemed to remember something. I was set in a shed with piles of scraps of paper, documents, and an old man to tell me

36

what the words were. It was because of new taxes imposed by Cairo and tax gatherers who would be coming. I was to straighten it all out, then try to keep accounts of some sort. It was—very difficult, but better than the fields. I grew much stronger, though the food was always scanty."

"I have been wondering about your English," Lord Ingram broke in. "You could have heard none. Yet you speak well."

The serious face lighted. "Thank you, sir. I am glad. You see, I never lost it. I had to have something to hold to, to keep me sane, and, and myself. I knew I was thinking in English. I convinced myself that someday I would escape. Then I would need what I knew was my own language. Arabic was around me, I had to learn it. But whenever I could I kept thinking, talking to myself, in English. I tried to recite what I had once learned, to describe places that came into my mind, to stay awake at night and work at it." He stopped abruptly. "Forgive me for going on so. But it was the one thing I had to cling to and I tried never to abandon my efforts. When I was too weary I fell into despair. But I would make myself start again."

"You were most wise. It must have taken a great effort of will to keep at it so. What made you run away?"

"The sherif's eldest son returned from a long expedition far to the south. He brought back quantities of goods to trade, ivory, black slaves, cloth, much else. I was set to writing it all down and the prices he said he had paid. His father wished to keep track. But the son did not like a written record. He changed his figures each day. I told his father. That infuriated them both. My ancient friend warned me that evening. While serving he had heard the son convince the sherif that I was dangerous, knew too much. I must be killed for their safety. That night I left. I knew I should follow the river as it flowed. At times there had been gossip, laughter, about foreigners who had come, after the armies had departed, to look for antiquities. Once I heard there was a mad Englishman living in a tomb above Luxor. I knew I must find him. So I ran at night and hid by day and stole food when I could find it."

"A most horrifying experience." Lord Ingram looked away from the grave, chiseled face. Chris let out a long sigh. She knew enough to realize a little how much had been omitted from the quiet account. "You showed great fortitude and skill," her father went on. "I am sure you will recover soon what portions of your memory are now obscured. Of course you must stay with us until we settle what is to be done. But now, Chris, we must get to work."

Inspiration came to her. "Have you any skill in drawing, Sidi? If you have you might help us."

He spread his hands, a gesture he must have picked up. "I do not know. I am happy to try."

"Good. Help will be welcome." Lord Ingram rose and carried his stool to the dining table and led the way to the tomb.

The pictures on the walls of the first two rooms stopped Sidi. "The colors are so bright . . . it is all so full of life . . . so much is happening . . ." he exclaimed. "I seem to remember no one can read the writings, those markings . . ."

"It is to that end we are working," Lord Ingram told him briskly. "These have been copied, as far down as the sand permits. We are now on the second series."

Again Sidi gazed with astonishment. "These . . . the private life of the personage . . . they are so happy."

Chris started to climb the heap of sand. In a flash he was beside her, mounting, holding out both hands, one to take the jug, one to take hers and give her a tug to the top. "That is much better," she gasped, and made her way to a corner while her father welcomed the same help. When he was standing firmly he pulled from his pocket a pad and stick of charcoal.

"See that cartouche?" He pointed to an oval line surrounding figures and strange marks. "See if you can copy that. Take your time. Accuracy is the first essential. These are for scholars, we must always remember."

Sidi nodded and planted his feet firmly. They worked in silence as the sun shone through the open roof of the hall. Chris moved and sand slid under her feet and again when she made a hole for the jug. "Drat," she said loudly.

Sidi lowered his pad. "May I make a suggestion?" he asked diffidently. "If we could obtain some kind of planks to stand on I believe we could work more easily; the sand would not slide so much."

"Excellent. I should have thought of that myself. But I doubt if we have any wood." He peered at the pad the other held, praised it, and put him on another cartouche.

"I'll go to Luxor this afternoon," Chris offered. "We need more food anyway and Ali can find some boards."

It seemed a particularly hot trip on the road and Chris was glad to throw back the hood of the galabia and loosen its folds when she returned to the studio. Both men were bent over the worktable. That meant her father had accepted Sidi as assistant. How sad it was at the end of the stay! "Ali bought some wood for three piasters," she told them brightly, not hesitating at all to interrupt their concentration, "and a mat for Sidi to sleep on. I found some more mutton and three chickens, not plucked, and maize and lentils and fruit. And I did not spend above half of the money you gave me, Father."

His eyes twinkled at her. "A good, provident manager, as always. We will count on two feasts."

The dinner was praised by all three men and Chris went quite pink with pleasure, though of course Ali had done the cooking. Sidi went to speak to Ali when it was over. Chris wondered uneasily what Ali would make of a foreigner speaking the local dialect or whatever it was and hoped his curiosity would not extend to such matters.

"He seems a decent chap," Sidi remarked as he settled his stool beside theirs where a breeze came from the river.

"He is better than most," Lord Ingram allowed, "but almost all Arabs are devious, unreliable, deceitful, thievish, and quite without what we regard as morals. I confess I chose him for his open face. Then I brought him here, told him if any of our things were missing when we left I would send word to the bey at Luxor, and reminded him that the bastinado was one favorite form of punishment. If all is well he is to get a good baksheesh when we leave. In the meantime I pay him four piasters a day, which is high pay and delights him."

"I asked him if he heard any news in the souk," Chris put in. "I could not understand much but I am sure he did say that the foreign officer on horseback had left with his men."

"Good." Her father nodded. "I was hoping I would not have to evade his questions. Since that danger is removed I think we should leave quite soon. With the help of our new assistant we will finish more quickly than I anticipated. Also, the panoramas in the second set of rooms, hunting in the marshes, floating on the Nile, harvesting, being entertained, are more spacious, not so crowded with figures. The first rooms, so crowded with figures and writings, the battle and the soldiers, the prisoners brought to the king, the processions of priests, were quite difficult to reproduce accurately. I will go to Luxor and begin to enter negotiations for a boat to take us to Boulak. We will go to the house of the hospitable Mr. Winton and to the consul in Cairo for more funds.

"As for our new friend," he turned to his left, "I have been giving some thought to your sad case. It is self-evident you must return to England. So I propose you go down the river with us, to Alexandria, and to England. It might be helpful if you would take a hand at an oar or sail, or assist in carrying, but I trust you would not object."

"Of course not, sir." Sidi let out a great sigh. "You are so very kind. I will do anything."

The dark head nodded. "I was sure. I confess I will be glad to have the consul put me in touch with the representative of Coutts's so I can draw out more funds. It is not comfortable to become short of funds in a foreign land. Splendid. Now let us to work. Christina, since you feel you cannot accurately match colors by lantern light perhaps you could do some simple transferring for us."

"Father!" Her tone was so outraged both men jumped. "You must know I had drawing lessons as well as painting when I was in school! You should have asked me long ago. I am quite good at it."

"Sorry, my dear. I had forgotten that was one of your many accomplishments," he said meekly. "Then we will finish..."

"I have looked at the boards Ali brought," Sidi said. "They are thin but I think they will hold us."

"The only boards we can buy are thin." The older man rose. "They are from the cases that have held mummies. There is almost no other wood available."

"Oh, I say, sir!" The protest was startled.

"Sad but true. The first time we needed a fire Ali brought some parts of the mummies themselves and was rather miffed when I refused to have them used for cooking and sent him for something else. He brought dried cornstalks, which are really not adequate." He vanished into the studio.

"Burning mummies!" Sidi looked more disturbed than Chris had seen him.

"It's all they have, they say," she explained kindly. "It is indeed a startling thought. But there are countless pits just filled with mummies, said to be of the lower and middle classes, and more pits are found constantly on both sides of the river. It seems only sensible to the fellaheen to burn what is available."

The three boards, gingerly placed the next morning, did give better footing and made the copying easier. At the end of the day Lord Ingram declared he was so pleased he would go to Luxor the next morning.

Over the chickens Sidi asked hesitantly, "How did you come to choose this particular tomb to copy, sir? I seem to know there are many great temples and tombs in the land and this is small."

"But this is mine," Lord Ingram told him with some pride. "I found it. No one had been in it since the robbers emptied it so many countless years ago. And I was charmed by it."

"But how did you come to be here?"

"Four of us, after Oxford, made the grand tour. In Rome we heard travelers talk of Egypt and its marvels. We went back to reading Herodotus and were fired. The difficulties and dangers appealed to us. We went to Cairo, hired a boat, and came upriver, stopping everywhere we could get ashore. We stayed in Thebes. The temples of Luxor and Karnak greatly impressed us. One afternoon in search of some exercise, I walked alone up the road, left it, pushed through the greenery to the sand high above it, and followed the cliffs. By pure chance I noticed a pile of tumbled rocks and a hole beside it, a black hole. I went back to the nearest village, paid two men to come with torches and push aside some stones and go inside with me. I was amazed and enchanted, and of course agreed with the men it was empty and useless, and left, feeling this tomb was peculiarly mine. I told my friends I had found an empty tomb, which held no interest for them as they were seeking some souvenirs to carry home. I told myself I would come back."

Looking a little embarrassed, he halted. "Well, the best plans often must be postponed. For years I did nothing about it. Last summer, talking with my old friend Freddy Lethbridge, who is, among other things, a trustee of the British Museum, about the linguists endeavoring to decipher that trilingual stone—how fortunate one of the languages is Greek—I thought of *my* find. I advanced the suggestion I come to Egypt, since I was free of obligations, and copy some of the wall paintings and inscriptions. He became most enthusiastic. The more I thought about it the more I felt a desire to return to this strange land. So I did. It has been a pleasure," and he beamed affectionately at Chris, "made the more so since she insisted on accompanying me."

She smiled back with affection. "Now I am grown I couldn't let you go off alone. If I had it would have meant another year at that school, which I did not need in the least."

"I can understand how this one seized your fancy," Sidi nodded, "but the great temples must be magnificent."

"I was mildly tempted, at times. We stopped at Abydos, Dendera, both very handsome, and those of Karnak and Luxor are awe-inspiring. But they are so crowded, filled so with huts, shacks, people, sand, that much is hidden. Why, the great temple across the river at Edfu has a whole village in its courtyard and is surrounded. There is an Arab village right on the roof of the temple at Dendera and untold families living inside and around it. At any of them I would have been surrounded myself by beggars, the curious, screaming children. I could not have worked in any comfort. We investigated the valley of the dead across the river, fascinating but impossible to work there."

"My favorite object in all Egypt is the dear Sphinx," Chris remarked dreamily. "You feel she is looking all the way to the Atlantic, and is so lonely."

"And I confess to a weakness for the pyramids," Lord Ingram chuckled. "I have no liking for Napoleon, but he made a memorable phrase when he told his soldiers camped around them that forty centuries were looking down upon them. But—no pictures there. And if we had stayed in Luxor we would have been forced to live quite differently at greater expense. My patience would have been tried beyond my endurance, in spite of my daughter's efforts to manage for me. It has been most satisfactory here. And no one is interested in the mad Englishman who merely copies drawings on walls instead of seeking to dig up statues to take with him and will not be cozened into those found by the fellaheen or recently made and passed off as ancient. But with money running low and time too, for the cloudy days are approaching, we should be leaving.

"But I have talked more than I intended." He looked from one to the other apologetically. "Have I exhausted you for the evening or could you do a little work?"

They could, and became so absorbed time passed unnoticed.

Chapter Four

Soon after sunrise Lord Ingram left with Ali, who approved of visits to the town. Sidi asked to be allowed to try his hand at copying figures as well as hieroglyphics and Christina said she would get on with her coloring. She was about to go for her paintbox when Sidi touched her arm. "This would be a good time to make the false bottom for your chest, if you permit."

When the chest was empty he carried it to the daylight and Chris sat down with the small bag of golden objects. One by one she spread them on the stone step. How charming they were, and so beautifully made! The long-legged ibis, head uplifted, she admired particularly. But the others were so appealing—the owl looked aloofly wise, the cat enigmatic, the fox haughty, the lamb trusting. The snake and the crocodile she put to one side and touched the goose and the flying duck. "Aren't they lovely!" she exclaimed to Sidi beside her, trying to cut down a board with a knife. "And they match the sketches I made, I'm sure." She went for her own rolls. "See? I'm sure they were once toys."

"Very likely. Yes, and," picking up one and weighing

it in his hand, "I am sure they are good solid gold. I take it you did not tell your father about them?"

"No," she admitted. "He is so honorable, and so generous. I am selfish. I wish to keep them."

"Of course. You are right. But it is regrettable there is not more jewelry."

"Yes, but this is a complete set. Someday I will wear it to a ball, for in truth I have only my mother's pearls."

"And very becoming they will be."

Looking up in surprise she found he was staring at her.

"You are very pretty," he went on thoughtfully. "I had not realized, had not really looked, perhaps. There are flecks in your eyes I had not noticed. They are more, is the word hazel, than gray. In the sun your hair has lights in it. And when you smile your eyes dance."

"Why, why, you are kind," she stammered. No one had praised her face before and she had never given it much thought, knowing it was not beautiful.

"I do not think I am kind. I only say what I see. But perhaps it is not proper to speak so to a young lady, for you were startled. I have forgotten so much. You are not offended?" The blue eyes were anxious.

"How could I be when you say such nice things?" She knew she was blushing and dropped her eyes. "But girls are taught to be embarrassed when given compliments."

"I would not embarrass you," he said solemnly, "if that makes you uncomfortable."

"Not very." She laughed a little. "I—I enjoy it. But it is my turn. You are looking much better. You have, as is said, good bones, but they are no longer so obvious. Your eyes are such a deep blue they are quite striking. You will be nice-looking when that beard is gone."

"That is good to hear. I am not embarrassed." He

laughed with her. His hair without the turban looked very white.

It caught her attention and she gazed at him thoughtfully. "You will look even better when your hair is no longer white."

"I do not know what I can do about that." He went back to working on the board.

"Nor I." She poked at the lamb. "Perhaps if you are ever in a position not to see people you could have it cut off right down to the skin and hope it will come in the right color."

"I will remember. Let us see if this board fits. I chose one with some lines of color so it will look more like the bottom of the chest. I am still unhappy when I think of its first use, but this is better than burning it."

With a little more cutting it fitted neatly so one small scallop was cut out at one side so it could be lifted out at need. The animals and jewelry were spread on a bed of leaves from the reeds and then covered in the hope they would not make a sound when moved and the board fitted in place. They both looked at it proudly. He carried the chest back into her room to be filled. On her table lay her scissors.

When he had placed the chest she took his arm. "Come outside. I am going to cut your beard."

He jumped away. "No. I know that is not fitting," and hurried to the entrance.

Laughing, she pursued him and caught his arm. "You must let me. I do Father's beard and hair, too. If he can support the ignominy you can. Your beard is much too thick and wide and does not match what you are wearing. Sit down."

He gave her a hunted look and started away but at her tug collapsed on the step. "Please, no," he pleaded.

"Shut your eyes. You will not be so afraid. Think

how much easier it will be to wash your face without so much curly hair around it. Ready-set-go." With a delighted gurgle she began to chip away at the curls on the right-hand side. She would have liked to make the beard pointed and neat, as her father's was square and neat, but knew that would not do. So she cut it shorter and then took out patches so the effect was scraggly and uneven. She began to laugh again before she was half through.

"Please," he pleaded. "Your hand will slip."

"It will if you talk and waggle your chin. Quiet, now." At last she backed away and cocked her head on one side. "A very expert cut," she announced gleefully. "You can open your eyes. Here is my mirror so you can admire yourself."

Rather shamefacedly he took the mirror, peered from all sides, and handed it back. "It *is* better," and he blushed. "But now I will feel strange." Suddenly he laughed. "Thank you, Miss Kelway. Now, could I not cut your hair? There is so much of it and the curls would make it difficult, but I would like to try."

In her turn she backed away. Her father had not offered to do that and it certainly was longer than usual. But the risk was too great. "You are kind to offer," she told him airily, "but I like it long. And now you see the improvement I made you must let me trim every two weeks."

His eyes crinkled at the corners. "It was pleasant to feel your fingers. That I did not expect. Anytime you may cut, Miss Kelway, for you are truly expert." And they laughed together.

Lord Ingram announced that in six days they would board a dahabieh at Luxor. Chris had thought she would be glad to leave the discomforts of life in the storehouse and the encircling sand, but when she went to say good-by to Clio's tomb and stood for the last time between the lotus-topped pillars and looked up to the two foxlike creatures carved on the lintel she found tears in her eyes. The pictures now seemed like old friends she was leaving. She hoped no one would ever come to the tomb again.

Sidi showed his practical ingenuity again by suggesting he wrap the rolls of the pictures in reeds tied with vines to protect them which would be stronger than cloths. A smaller one was kept separate for the Pasha. He also oversaw the packing and transporting of bundles, chests, boxes, since all the household goods would be needed on the boat and probably on the ship, for many were not well provided for passengers.

In spite of his baksheesh Ali wept loudly when they parted at the dahabieh, which made the crew at first nod approvingly then join in his lamentations and praise of the noble lord as they pushed into the river.

"It all came to more than I had hoped," confessed the noble lord when they were settled and sitting under the awning. "But it takes so long to interview and bargain with others and the bey assured me this reis is honest and knows the river. He insisted on four men, in case the wind fails, and a cook. Also I felt it wise to engage an interpreter. His name is Misreh and he seems agreeable and experienced. He wishes to return to Cairo so came at a small fee. Then there were the supplies, a sheep, chickens, vegetables, fruits with which to start the journey, but I have no doubt we will have to go ashore almost every day for more provisions. At least they are kept in the front of the boat with the crew ..."

Chris leaned over and patted his hand. "We are going to be very comfortable and well cared for. And our cabins in the hutlike contrivance behind us are larger than the others we had. And chairs to sit in!" She tossed back her hood and produced a wide-brimmed straw hat that matched those of the crew. "It will be welcome to wear a hat again. I wish I could get rid of this boring robe, but don't worry, I know I can't yet. This is going to be so enjoyable!" She patted his hand again and smiled at him.

Going down the Nile, with the two triangular sails in front that pointed in opposite directions and looked like wings, was even more pleasant than mounting it had been. The blue water and sky, the white sails of the feluccas mirrored in the river, the glimpses of life on the shores, all held endless fascination. Birds were everywhere, skimming the water, floating, flying from palm to palm. Proudly Misreh named some, storks and cranes lifting their feet high as they paraded, ducks paddling, herons and cranes swooping, and busy tiny birds he did not know. Crocodiles fringed the shores of small islands, lying close together in the sun. Women washed white clothes and hung them on green bushes and laughed together. Oxen, sheep, asses, camels could be seen often on the road. And above it all the tops of the palms, in fringes and in groups, moved gently and could only be likened to feather dusters, as every traveler admitted.

"I miss my work. I need some occupation," proclaimed Lord Ingram the second morning. "Christina, you and I have been separated too long. You have had a governess, two years at a highly recommended school at Bath. How much do you know?"

Astonished, she dropped her spoon on her melon. "I don't know," she answered, a little apprehensively.

"I am going to find out, for I would enjoy filling in any lacunae." He moved them to chairs under the awning and after an hour of seemingly random questions declared her French was quite good, her knowledge of English writings spotty but she would probably remedy that by her own reading, and what she knew of

English history seemed to begin and end with 1066. Her ignorance of Latin he deplored, but at her heated protest allowed girls did not need that. He would concern himself with history and began forthwith, going back to the Celts and the Saxons. Thereafter, for an hour each morning and each afternoon he recounted what had happened in her country and Chris acknowledged he made it more interesting than any novel.

Sidi came and sat with them during those hours, listening intently, never speaking. Some of his time he spent with the reis or the interpreter, improving his Arabic, he said seriously, for one never knew when it might be useful. Often he took a turn at an oar.

One morning at the end of the lesson Lord Ingram spoke to him directly. "I have been thinking on your dilemma, my boy, and how you may go about discovering who you are. You must come and stay with us at Scure Priory and there we will plan your strategy."

"You are eternally kind, sir." Sidi hesitated. "I have thought about what to do in England but as yet I have no idea."

"Perhaps between now and then the needed names will come to you. Even one will give you a clue. Do not be concerned. Between us you will find yourself."

"It is my hope I may someday repay all you have done for me." Sidi stood up and bowed.

Lord Ingram watched the tall figure make its way to the bow. "He'll come about," he said comfortably. "He is intelligent and ingenious and well mannered. I hope it happens quickly."

It was during the fifteen days of the voyage to Cairo that Chris fell into an easy friendship that made life on the dahabieh particularly agreeable. On the third morning, while she sat on the bench by the gunwale watching a water buffalo being ridden down the bank by two small children, Sidi came to her and held out two balls of string. "Would you care to try fishing, Miss Kelway? Your father spoke of a lack of variety in our menus and the reis says fish can be easily caught and are very good. I found some string and hooks when I went ashore marketing with him. He tells me anything will do for bait, for the fish are innocent."

Eagerly she reached for one ball. "How diverting! I'd love to fish. It's been so long. A grain of maize will really lure one? The stone sinkers are fast to the line?" She whirled on the bench and tossed her line as far as she could, looked back to watch, and gaped as Sidi, apparently without thought, swung his bait around his head and hurled it toward the center of the stream.

"Good throw," praised Lord Ingram from under the awning.

"I'm better with a rod," Sidi said absently, as if that would be obvious. "These fish are truly ignorant of anything but a net. I have a bite."

While watching him haul in a dark flapping object Chris lost one fish but caught the second and pulled it up. She started to grasp it and remove the hook as usual but halted and stretched out hands and fish. "Won't you take it off for me?" she begged, a little plaintively.

"Delighted." He seized the fish. Glancing shame-facedly toward her father she saw his look of surprise and then a wide grin. After all, a girl could properly be timid on the right occasion...

When they had caught enough for crew and passengers it was quite natural to drop down under another piece of awning and begin to talk, first about the river, then about fishing, and when she mentioned fly fishing his face lighted and in a minute he said he remembered about that. His shyness melted and his hesitation at showing his ignorance and in a day or so he was asking questions, listening, nodding, saying he remembered

52

more and more. He would not speak of his time with Ibn-El-Hahir, but in the evening, after the three had talked and watched the stars and she had gone to her cabin she could hear their voices and was sure they were discussing many of those topics not felt proper for young ladies to hear. They all grew more tanned and Chris wondered if hers would ever fade and lamented she would never have the so-admired strawberries and cream complexion, and felt scarcely comforted when her father held that was too common and insipid for her. Sidi, she could not but notice, steadily looked less gaunt, and once, as she was turning the rag he had been wearing around his head into a round cap, she wondered what he would look like without the beard. He had admitted solemnly, his eyes dancing, that she had been right to cut it to match those around him. He was such an easy, comfortable man to be with it was like having a most companionable older brother. He would enliven the long sea voyage as he had the descent on the dahabieh.

One day she asked him if he was remembering more of his past. He did not look from his line but nodded. "Yes. Between you and your father and all you discuss and his lectures on the past, I do recollect more. Sometimes just one word will open up a whole chain of memories." He turned and gave her a brilliant smile. "In time, I will know all. Then I can take up my life."

Two days out of Cairo they had a hint of trouble. Sidi reported that the reis had picked up some floating tales of uneasiness in the city and a rising hostility to the English, but he had not heard the cause.

Though Chris would have liked to stop and admire the Sphinx and the pyramids again, her father felt the time should not be wasted, so they sailed on to Boulak, just below Cairo and its port. Mr. Winton was not happy to see them, though he allowed they were wise to leave the country. It was being spread that because Mahomet Ali had become friends with the French, England was planning to invade Egypt to assist the group of beys who opposed him. The rumors were enough to set off a volatile people against anyone who appeared English. Lord Ingram left immediately with Misreh for the office of the British consul in Cairo. Chris spent the afternoon washing her hair and trying to revive her English clothes while Mrs. Winton droned on about the difficulties of housekeeping in Boulak and the vagaries of the foreign residents.

Her father was thoughtful when he returned. Mr. Ackworth had confirmed that there were indeed rumors of an English descent planned for the spring. Funds were lacking at the consulate. One banker had been approached but had claimed to have no monies. An appointment had been made with the Pasha for the following noon and his help might be enlisted, and there were other bankers, but it was awkward. Mr. Winton would take a note, but they must get to Alexandria and then find passage. The Wintons made consoling sounds and Sidi slipped away and was absent at dinnertime, a tactful solving of a social dilemma.

Chris was on watch the next afternoon when her father, slumped on the donkey, supported by Sidi and Misreh, came through the gateway to the little courtyard. The two men carried him into the room and laid him on the pile of rugs. "What . . . ?" she stammered, for his face was gray and twisted in pain.

"Brandy," he gasped.

Swiftly Sidi brought a glass, propped him, held him up to drink it, while Chris knelt, speechless, and Misreh wrung his hands.

"Sorry," gasped her father. "Don't know what." He sipped at the brandy. "Chris." His hand groped for hers.

"Must tell you. Pasha rude. Took roll. No thanks. Served an ice." He twisted a little. "No help on money. Told me to leave country. Went to two bankers. More ices. No money. We have little left."

Misreh and Sidi spoke and Misreh ran from the room. "Try to rest, sir," Sidi said. "Misreh has gone for the finest physician in Boulak. And Mr. Winton will help us."

Lord Ingram's body gave a jerk and twisted in pain. "May be poison," he gasped. "Pasha uses it. More brandy. Must speak."

Chris sat very still. She could manage some things but she knew nothing about illness. She looked at the calm, intent face across from her. "Sidi," she whispered, "help us. I don't know what to do."

"The physician will tell us," he murmured and brought more brandy.

Her father sipped it, opened his eyes. "Pull me up straight," he directed. "Must speak to you both." He moved his head and looked at Sidi, his voice stronger. "You have remembered your name. I saw it on the boat. Your face lighted up. What is it?"

"I did not realize you noticed. I believe it is Derwent, Kirby Derwent. The names came suddenly while you were speaking of Charles the Second, and I *knew*."

"Good. Now, if I die Chris is left here alone. You must marry her, now. Then you can protect her, get her home safely. Sorry to say it, but you owe it to us."

"No!" Chris cried. "Father . . . it's not right . . ."

"Be still. Only thing. Sidi, you agree? Good. Find some paper. I'll do a note. There's a consul here. He's to bring license. There. Hurry."

Ignoring the hand Chris stretched out from her place by her father, Sidi took the note and passed Misreh and the turbaned physician at the door. The physician felt

55

and touched and looked grave and produced two twisted papers holding powders.

"What does he say?" Chris implored Misreh.

"He cannot tell the cause of milord's illness. Some such are very obscure. It is something within. The powders, in water, will ease the pain. He will pray to Allah that milord will reach his home safely. I must go and escort him to his house."

There was nothing Chris could do but bathe her father's face and hold his hand and listen to his labored breathing. Then Sidi was ushering in a short anxious Englishman while Misreh hovered as if to prevent his escape. Obviously summoning his strength, and aided by more brandy, Lord Ingram explained the consul's duty, dictated the names to go on the license, the place and date, sent for Mr. Winton to be a witness, and propping himself on one elbow directed Christina and Sidi to stand before him and the consul.

"It is simple," the consul explained nervously. "You repeat after me what I say. I have only done this three times...Now..."

Her eyes on her father's white face, Christina repeated words she scarcely heard or understood and heard the man beside her repeating similar phrases in a grave voice. Then, at a little table with a candle she was signing her name, as was Sidi, the consul, Mr. Winton, and at the bottom her father unsteadily put "Ingram." A bemused Mr. Winton invited them all for some wine, which was refused by her and her father.

"There," gasped Lord Ingram, letting himself down slowly. "Best I could think of to do. He'll take care of you. Chris, take that paper, keep it safely, hang it around your neck, you may need it if any trouble..." He gave a little moan and doubled up. She ran for a little of the powder and a mug. Then Sidi was taking it from her, propping up her father to drink the dose, and saying, "Sir, can you hear me?"

"Yes." One hand came up, the eyelids fluttered and opened. "Good boy. Feel better with Chris safe."

"But we may not be, sir. We must leave now. The reis and Misreh agree. There were mutterings in the streets as we passed. I heard them also. You are English, they say, and so you must be taking gold, treasures home with you. Misreh heard a man telling the Pasha you must be held, made to tell where is the gold, kept as a hostage for when the English attack."

Lord Ingram moved his head feebly. "Tonight? I can't walk."

"We'll carry you. The Pasha's men might come. The reis still has his crew. He will take us. Mr. Winton advises it, for your sake and your daughter's."

"Will go if you agree." The words fell slowly and stopped.

"He's fainted. Get everything together, Miss Kelway. I'll be back with the litters."

In a half hour he returned with the reis and litters. It was dark and windy at the river. Chris could hardly believe she was actually leaving Egypt. She could have been sorry but now felt only relief and anxiety. Her father was carried quickly to his cabin.

As she made to follow Sidi halted her at the entrance. "The reis agrees that milord will be very ill tonight. Do not come in no matter what you hear."

"I must be with my father." She tried to push him aside but it was like pushing at a stone wall.

"Not now." He caught her hands. "Believe me, you should not be in there. I will care for him." He pulled aside the rug hanging at her door. "Trust me, and stay here." There came the sound of a strange moan and Sidi raced away.

She sat down on her chest. He had promised, of

course, she could trust him. Her presence would embarrass them. She lay down and went into an uneasy sleep filled with strange sounds and the jiggling slap and bounce of an awkward boat meeting hard little waves.

The voyage to Alexandria was not pleasant. When the wind rose the waves tilted the awkward craft; when it failed all rowed. The river was crowded with boats of all types; any one of them might hold soldiers of the Pasha. When a shower descended the cook refused to make hot food for it was obviously the will of Allah that their food should be cold. In spite of it all her father improved a little each day. He had been horridly ill, he confessed, and would have been lost without their friend. At Alexandria the crew took a solemn farewell of the noble milord and the reis, departing with most of the remaining money, promised eternal devotion.

The three moved into the house of Mr. Birk, a merchant. Frankly Lord Ingram laid out their situation.

Mr. Birk shook his head. "There is only one ship sailing for England, the *Mary M.* for Plymouth, departing tomorrow. The cabins are taken but perhaps you could double up. Captain Listly is a good seaman but a hard man. No matter if I endorsed your note he would not take you and your belongings on board unless the passage was paid in hard money. And no banker here has any reserves."

"But another ship? We cannot stay here without funds," Lord Ingram protested shakily.

Again Mr. Birk shook his head. "No other ship for England is due. We will be happy to have you remain with us as long as necessary," he added in a voice that denied his words. "I will send your dinner. Tomorrow I will seek Captain Listly and present your case, though I have little hope."

They ate what they could, tried to make plans cheerfully, and lay down to try to sleep. Sidi had vanished.

Early in the morning her father sent for her. He was sitting up, his eyes brighter. "We are saved, my dear, by Sidi! He has brought me money, enough for the whole passage. He says it is a matter between him and some Arabs and I am not to concern myself about it."

Behind her she heard Sidi moving, gathering boxes and rolls. "How wonderful!" she breathed.

"Indeed it is. Mr. Birk has gone again to the captain to make sure no one else is taken on board. We must go to the ship as soon as possible, so get ready. We cannot thank our friend enough."

"Truly we cannot." She hurried off, pausing to whisper "I am so grateful" as she passed the white-clad figure tying up a roll of rugs.

He managed their breakfast, the litters, the porters in such a decisive manner that Chris was left a little in awe, for in spite of his garb all obeyed him. With the aid of Mr. Birk, the passage matter was settled: Lord Ingram would share a cabin with a young Mr. Smullens, Christina one with his wife. Mrs. Smullens instantly confided to Chris that she was pregnant and terrified of the voyage and could not wait to reach Nottingham. Seeing one box and the chest safely into the cabin, Chris hurried up on deck to join her father and Sidi at the rail.

Now they were about to sail she felt relief and gladness. "I do so thank you again," she said impulsively and laughed up to the aquiline face, "but I know I'll say that often these next weeks."

"Our friend here does not sail with us," her father told her unhappily. "I cannot persuade him."

"You are recovering, sir, and no longer have need of me. I have my private search to pursue, and must do it my own way, however long it takes. You can understand that," he pleaded.

"Of course." There was a sigh. "But I may be of assistance. When you reach Plymouth go to Dunlap's stables, hire a coach, put it on my account, and come to Scure Priory, near Methanbury, in Wilts. You will be most welcome, and we will plan together."

"You are kind, sir, but..."

"But I do not understand," Christina broke in, bewildered. "Why can't you come with us? We will need you, we so enjoy your company..." She had pushed back her hood and the wind was blowing her hair around her face so she put up one hand to hold it.

Sidi's expression was stern. He shook his head. "You are kind, Miss Kelway. But I must discover the man I believe betrayed me and who I am."

"We will be hard put to it to get along without you. And I will miss you." She put one hand on his arm as though to hold him. "I have enjoyed these past weeks." She felt tears in her eyes and blinked.

"Never can I repay what you, sir, and you, Miss Kelway, have done for me." Though he spoke unevenly his voice rang. He raised his arm and kissed her hand, dropped it, shook hands with her father, and hurried to the gangplank.

"Oh," Christina mourned. "I'm so sorry. Do you think he can manage alone?"

"Yes." Her father put an arm around her shoulder. "That young man will manage very well alone. I look forward to seeing him again. I will stay on deck a little. Why not look to your cabin now and then join me?" He reached for her hand and held it a moment. "You are a good companion. I could not have done without you, my dear."

She found a smile and squeezed his hand and looked to the dock, seeking one more sight of the tall white figure, but it had vanished. So she went below to see how she might stow her belongings in the tiny space. Her chest she pushed into one corner and sat down abruptly. Sidi was gone. But her hand stole to the front of the galabia she still wore and felt the little cloth bag she had fashioned. What was she? For the first time she realized none of them had mentioned that quick, lamplit occurrence in Boulak. Was she truly married to a man whose name might be Kirby Derwent? She had a document, ill printed and rather flimsy but definite, that said she was. Certainly she did not feel she was. In her deep fear for her father she had forgotten that happening. The two men must have also. Would it be forgotten forever? Yes, if this Kirby Derwent never appeared in her life again. And if he did, what sort of a man might he be? There was every chance he would wish to forget it. If he did not, her father would know how those few words could best be dissolved, obliterated. She would forget it herself, hide the paper, and assure herself there would be no consequences of her father's loving anxiety on her behalf. Hastily she took the little bag from around her neck, delved down in her chest, raised the false bottom, and thrust the bag beneath. Those few minutes had seemed quite unreal at the time. They were almost unbelievable now and could be buried in the bottom of her mind. But, she paused, she had so enjoyed those days on the dahabieh and Sidi's company. She *could* miss him if she allowed herself to dwell on that time. But she must not. She must wait for him to come to Scure Priory.

Chapter Five

The gray stone house known as Scure Priory, made from the monastery presented negligently by King Hal to his friend Kelway, was a more welcome sight than even the Eddystone Light had been. The voyage had tried the Kelways' endurance and patience, for the winds were contrary, the food mediocre, the captain and crew surly, and the storms of the notorious Bay of Biscay violent almost beyond belief. Christmas had passed practically unnoticed, for it arrived in the midst of unremitting rain and wind. Although her father had recovered from the illness at Boulak, which he was convinced had been caused by poison, both he and Christina were weary to the bone when they disembarked at Plymouth.

After taking a week to renew their forces, Lord Ingram set out for London, leaving Chris the quite congenial task of supervising the cleaning of the house and setting it in order. In the midst of so many tasks Egypt faded further away. Her father returned in another week, wearing a new suit and carrying a glow of satisfaction. At dinner he refused to open his satchel of news and demanded hers. Except for calls on tenants, she had only made the obligatory visit to Lady Effington, the social arbiter of the county. She had evinced no interest in Egypt, had told Chris she was too scrawny, should thank her stars every day she had a wave in her hair so it did not matter how badly she treated it, should put curds and lemon juice or vinegar on her face to whiten it, and then repeated the gossip of the past months, which was quite dull. Her father, highly amused, shooed her into the library and joined her quickly.

"Now, what have you been doing?" she demanded quickly.

"So much, my dear, I can hardly credit I was recently the forlorn creature who disembarked at Plymouth. The first evening in town I went of course to call on Freddy Lethbridge. I carried just one roll of the paintings, the one of Richard in his war chariot. He was astounded, delighted, congratulated me, called in Letty, Lady Lethbridge, who was extravagant in her praise. He promised he would carry it the next day to Lord Frampton—he is president of the Society of Antiquaries, Chris—and consult where the rolls should go to be of greatest assistance to the scholars working on the translations. I must confess I was more pleased than if I had just won a race at Newmarket with a hopeless horse.

"Two days later—in the meantime I ordered some clothes, you'll be glad to hear—he had me to dinner. Letty is a charming woman, by the way, and the dinner was excellent. He told me instantly Lord Frampton was deeply impressed by my roll. A special meeting of the Society is to be called in my honor so I may display the collection and relate how they were made. I confess I had hoped for something like this. It is an honor, you know, to speak to the Society no matter what one's standing, or achievements. I told of you, and your invaluable assistance. The collection will redound to Freddy's credit, too, since we planned it all together."

"I'll be so proud when you speak," Chris burst out.

He shook his head. "Sorry, my dear, but you won't hear me. The Society is quite rigid. No ladies at the meetings and only at one evening reception a year, when the barriers are lowered. But I will recount all to you. So, I went on to speak of you. They both, of course, knew your dear mother so they had a particular interest and it gave me great pleasure to tell them all you had done."

"Was London beautiful?" Chris asked wistfully.

"It was wet and dreary. But, to continue my tale. We joined Letty in the saloon, very tastefully done in green. I was delighted to see two black marble sphinxes, erroneously on long legs, supporting the white marble top of one of the tables. I am not, I would have you know, entirely unacquainted with ladies and their needs." He cocked his head on one side and chuckled. "I had had it in mind you would require a new wardrobe and someone to guide you to the best shops. I spoke of this. Letty exclaimed with delight. Of course, you would need, and obviously deserve, a complete new outfit. There was nothing she enjoyed more than shopping and she had had such few opportunities of late. Her only daughter was married ten years ago, very satisfactorily, but is now buried in the wilds of Northumberland with four children. She promptly extended an invitation to you to come and visit her while you refurbished."

"How kind." Chris was doubtful. "Will she tell me what I should buy and wear at every point?"

"Oh, I think not. She is amiability itself, a little heavyset now, perhaps, but of a laughing humor and interested in everything. She fell silent after that offer for quite five minutes and then interrupted Freddy. I had inspired her to do her duty, she declared, which was so often disagreeable but not in this case. Freddy has a sister in Sussex who has a daughter about eighteen. In November Amelia hinted openly that Audrey was at just the age when she would benefit most from the delights of a London season, to which her mother, because of her delicate health, could not introduce her. Letty had ignored the hints, for her sister-in-law is about as delicate as a heifer, and as interesting, but Audrey had seemed a pleasant girl. London was more dull than not when one had nothing to occupy oneself. Therefore, Lady Lethbridge concluded, she would entertain herself, enjoy your company, and do her duty by having both you girls visit her for the season. I protested, it was too much. But she told me roundly two girls were much easier to care for than one, and now she had decided to do her duty you and I would be doing her a favor if you became her guest."

"Father!" Chris stared at him, eyes and mouth wide. "I never hoped for a season."

"I know you didn't, my dear, but I had hoped to manage it in one way or another and this way I am sure is the best. Letty is up to the nines and will put you in the way of everything. She has standing, and you could hardly enter society under more elevated auspices. I promised her you are pretty and well behaved and will obey her, so I trust you to see that I keep my word."

"Of course, dear, dear Father." She halted. "But how can I leave you here alone with only Mrs. Bemis to manage for you?"

"Oh, you won't." His tone was jaunty. "I rather fancy a turn at city living myself. And of course I would wish to be on hand when you join the polite world. I will put up at Grillon's. I have before. It is stuffy but comfortable, and at the moment comfort appeals to me enormously. And I will hope to be conferring about my rolls."

"And there is your appearance at the Society. It will be so good to have you in town, too. Father, how kind you are," and she rushed and kissed him again. "When do we leave?"

"Not for a week or so. I have been absent too long and must see to the estate, repairs for tenants, our own fields. The roads should be better then. Lady Lethbridge needs the time to settle matters with her sister-in-law, but you will have ample time to order your gowns before the season opens. She also assured me, with a laugh, that there would be no problem about vouchers for Almack's. It is my hope you will enjoy your visit enormously. Oh, and I gave her my word you were not on the prowl for a husband so she need have no concern about that."

"No, of course I am not." She was emphatic about that. "I am too happy to be home and with you at last. And when we return here I will do my best to see you are well cared for, though we will both always miss Mother most sadly."

"That is inevitable," he said quietly. "But we will enjoy ourselves as she would wish. Put on the best clothes you have and go calling around the county, for you will not have another chance for some time. I fear you will find few who will be interested in your experiences in Egypt. That reminds me to leave instructions that Sidi is to be told where to find me when he arrives, and advanced money if necessary. There is no telling in what state he may be. A mystery, that young man. I could not tell while he listened to my talks on the boat whether he was learning or refreshing what he had once known."

"But you believed his account," she said a little anxiously.

"I did, in spite of the vagueness as to how his misfortunes came about. What was he before—that is the mystery. Even in the state we found him he had charm and breeding, such as go with a born gentleman. But he might have turned into a wrong 'un, you know, a sharp, a swindler, anything. Somewhere, possibly during that time under the sherif, he learned to hold his face inscrutable. But we owe him a great deal, so I keep an open mind and you must also, and trust we will learn more when he comes, or soon thereafter. I look forward to seeing him."

"So do I," Christina agreed, and added vehemently, "a mystery is always aggravating."

"True, but unless it can be quickly solved it is best ignored or put aside and trust a solution will appear someday."

It was the mention of Sidi that sent her to her treasures. She had not forgotten them but she had been so busy. She felt she could not trust her father not to give them, or have her present them, to the Society of Antiquaries. All those stuffy men—they were sure to be stuffy—would sneer at the cat and the owl and put them in a drawer where they would never be seen. So the next afternoon, when the bare trees stood black along the hilltops and around the front lawn and the rain was too violent for riding, she drew her chest to the window seat.

First she paused to admire her own rolls of pictures, then felt for the scallop in the false bottom. With several creaks the thin wood came up to show the layer of dry leaves and the small white bag which she had stuffed down in one corner. Pushing aside the leaves she looked down with delight. The figures were not truly small, she decided, for they were at least three inches long and as gleaming and perfect as she remembered. She picked up the ibis and ran a finger down the

67

back while the cat stared back at her. She counted them over. Twelve. But there had been fourteen, she was sure, and went over them again. The two she had liked the least, the alligator and the snake, were missing.

Aghast, she stared at the array. Sidi had taken two. No one else knew of them or of the false bottom. That those two were gone was further proof. Desolation swept over her. How *could* he have taken them! She would gladly have given them to him as part of his share for finding them. When could he have opened her chest? She remembered the evening in Alexandria when he had disappeared while she was with her father. He might at least have asked her if he might have them. Perhaps he needed them—but he should have told her. Perhaps he would confess when he came to Scure Priory. That thought was cheering.

It was still winter when they went up to London, and the fire in the grate of the small rose saloon at Cavendish Square was no warmer than the welcome of Lady Lethbridge. By the time tea arrived she had turned to Christina, exclaiming how pretty she was, and though not the beauty her mother had been would compete very satisfactorily with all but the accredited. Her brown hair, such nice lights in it, would be charming when cut and arranged, her figure was a little thin perhaps but she was tall enough so she could not be overlooked, her eyes were her best feature as anyone could see, and the shape of her mouth offset the determination that the perceptive could discern in her chin. Only Sidi had ever praised her to her face, for her father always said she looked pretty to him at any time, and while she blushed at the outspoken words she reflected that praise did help establish confidence.

Her father just laughed, though in a pleased way,

and told Lady Lethbridge not to spoil the child and that if she ever developed the delightful charm of her hostess she would be fortunate indeed. That made the lady laugh with pleasure and say he had always been the most delicious flirt, and follow with an invitation to dinner that night. So, equally gratified, he had gone off to Grillon's.

When he had gone the two beside the tea table looked at each other calmly. Lady Lethbridge was on the plump side, but with a comfortable figure that went with the smile on her round face beneath the gray curls. Chris felt she would be agreeable to live with, to obey, and to enjoy. She started to say as much but Lady Lethbridge spoke first.

"I am delighted you have come to visit, my dear. I was not looking forward to another season of playing whist and listening to music with nothing to occupy my attentions. I brought out my own girl with great success, and though things are not quite the same I know I can see to it that you enjoy yourself. Your dear father says you are not on the lookout for a husband, which I confess is a relief as it removes a burden from the shoulders of any chaperone. Has any man ever engaged your affections?"

"Oh no, ma'am." Chris moved forward a little in her chair. "I was at school for several years. When I visited friends at times all the brothers seemed quite dull. I will be happy to be at home with my father, who is very good company when he is not busy."

"That I know. I can see you are well behaved and will set a good example to Audrey, if she needs it. I must thank you for enabling me to do my duty in such a pleasant way and yet feel uncommonly virtuous in the process. Audrey arrives tomorrow. She will call me Aunt Letty and I feel you must do the same so we can be cozily informal. I have put you two girls at the back of the house on the floor above. Mrs. Pritchett, the housekeeper, with us twenty years, will show you. You will discover I do not mount stairs unless it is essential for my pleasure or well-being. She has a young niece who wishes to learn to be an abigail who is coming in for the two of you and I promise you Mrs. Pritchett will see she learns quickly." She stopped and nodded, brown eyes alit. "We will deal well together, for you let me talk as I wish without interrupting, an attitude I approve." She rang a little golden bell set on the tea tray and a footman arrived before the echo had died. "Angus will show you up the stairs and Mrs. Pritchett will join you at the top. We will have sherry at eight in the green saloon. Until then, my dear."

Heartened by the tea and the monologue, Chris dipped a curtsy and followed Angus. There was one flight of stairs and then a beaming Mrs. Pritchett was showing her rooms overlooking what would be a garden. Her praise won an extra wide beam from the housekeeper.

Lord Lethbridge matched his lady wife, for he also had brown eyes that twinkled and though as tall as Lord Ingram was stockily built and must have looked formidable in his uniform. He put Chris at ease at once by expanding on his pride and pleasure at the success of the stay in Egypt. Her father reported that his room at Grillon's was all he could desire and the coming weeks could not but be delightful.

"You must drop in here whenever you are at a loose end for a dinner," Lady Lethbridge urged, "for now you are at last in town we mean to see all we can of you and Christina will wish to recount her doings."

"I intend to accompany you, ma'am, on occasion so I can view them myself and have the pleasure of dancing with you again," he retorted. At that Lord Lethbridge raised his glass. "Brave man," he bantered and all laughed.

After an exhilarating morning of having her hair cut quite short and strolling down Piccadilly and trying not to show her surprise at shops and people, Chris knew that she could not but enjoy the coming weeks. She wondered a little about Audrey but was reassured as soon as she set eyes on her. The girl might be called a little buxom, but not unduly, and was vivaciously pretty with golden hair and blue eyes and a complexion that made Chris wonder if the tan she had acquired from the sun had adequately faded. Audrey was also natural and unaffected, which was inevitable in a girl fresh out of school and Sussex.

In her room at first she was shy with Chris but an offer to help her unpack banished her hesitations. The unpacking revealed to Chris that Audrey's wardrobe was not quite so modish as her own and as scanty, which put her in charity with the girl. It was as well they were to start the next day acquiring new ones.

"You will find Lord and Lady Lethbridge very comfortable people," Chris began as they settled in her room for a coze until being summoned to tea. "But, I forgot. You are their niece, so you know them. I am to call Lady Lethbridge Aunt Letty, as you do."

"I do not know them well," Audrey explained, "for I have not seen them above four times in my life. I would never dare to call Lord Lethbridge uncle."

Chris laughed and agreed and before she could think of a fresh topic Audrey burst out, "Are you come to find a husband?"

"No." Chris was rather weary of the question. "My father wishes me to enjoy the season and Aunt Letty says she will see we do and that it is much easier for her if we are not on the prowl."

"I am so glad." She giggled a little. "You see, I am not, either. But Mother insists I am."

"But why?"

"Mother says I must see the world and meet a number of men before I settle on one. And above all that I must marry a man of a more elevated position than the son of Squire Purvis because I will be quite a considerable heiress."

There was so much in those sentences that Chris did not know which subject to approach, so she chose the last. "It must be pleasant to be an heiress." She felt no envy. She knew she would have an agreeable competence eventually and that seemed to her quite satisfactory.

"The fortune comes from a great-aunt for whom I was named. It does not do me any good at the moment because it will not come to me for nearly two years, until I am twenty. I have no idea what figure it will carry. And I do not see it matters." Audrey looked as if she were pleading for understanding but Chris felt that was beyond her at the moment. So she chose the other chief topic of interest. "What is wrong with the son of a squire?"

"There's nothing *wrong* with Jim. He's the most sought-after man in the county and his family is older than ours. But there's no title. Mother wants me to marry a title and have an establishment and be very modish, and all I wish is to marry Jim—we've known each other all our lives—and settle down on his estate and have babies and be happy."

"It is not surprising your mother wishes you to see more of the world first." Chris advanced the notion cautiously.

"No," Audrey agreed generously. "It is what she had and enjoyed herself hugely and is confident I will also. I'm not sure of that, for we are very different. But she was so *insistent,* and won my father to her way of thought, and when she said I could never see Jim again—though he did not agree to that *at all*—I could see nothing for it but to do as she wished and come to stay with Aunt Letty."

"You may enjoy it much more than you now believe," Chris told her with some confidence, for the girl was blond and pretty and would surely take, and if it were known she was an heiress she would be an object of attention. "That knock means tea is served. So come along and begin your visit with the most delicious cakes."

Chapter Six

Audrey turned out to be a practical girl as well as a pretty one, for she told Chris that though she deplored being separated from Jim she had decided to enjoy her time in London since such an event could occur only once in a lifetime, and of course nothing would alter her feelings in any degree. They both displayed an enthusiastic interest in their wardrobes and gowns, which gratified Lady Lethbridge and led her to make purchases of her own. When bonnets and gowns began to arrive she gaily told them she would be enjoying the affairs almost as much as they would.

In one aspect they were deficient. They did not waltz, nor know the newest versions of the country dances. To acquaint them, she announced at one luncheon, she had summoned Sir Gavin Hadley—his mother was a cousin—and his friend, Mr. David Bowman, to tea that afternoon.

"They are pleasing boys, as you will discover, down from Oxford, sensible enough to realize they have not the temperament nor the fortune to attempt to become tulips of the ton nor the physical prowess and wealth to become an out-and-out Corinthian. They are both aides to some member of Parliament, are welcome in society, and up-to-the-minute on everything necessary."

Both girls watched her with concern. Here would be the first test of the coming season. Suppose they could not learn to perform the dances with grace and aplomb!

"In exchange for a large tea they will gladly spend an hour showing you the dances and repeat as often as necessary. Also I will ask them, but only if you like them, my loves, to dine here and escort us to Lady Spofford's ball. It is so lowering to enter a ballroom and be compelled to stand at one side and wait for some man to be brought up to dance with you. This way you will have partners immediately and others will be then produced. So wear one of the new afternoon frocks this afternoon, for you wish to make a good impression."

The two young men were both pleasant and attractive, with manners beyond reproach. Sir Gavin had the darker hair and merry brown eyes and Mr. Bowman hair of an indeterminate brown and a more serious expression. Both professed themselves happy to make the girls acquainted with the latest dances and after a truly overwhelming tea they all repaired to the ballroom, where Lady Lethbridge, with zest and vigor, played the tunes requested. Since the girls knew already some of the older country dances they had little difficulty in acquiring "Gypsies at the Fair" and "A-Maying We Will Go," though all felt another lesson would be advisable. The waltz, so different in approach and dance, was another matter, but soon the *one,* two, three beat became familiar, as did the odd position of dancing while a man had his arm around one's waist. It was all so gay and lively they soon felt quite at home with each other. Another session was set for two days later. Then would come the first ball.

Sent to her room to nap before dressing for the ball, Chris lay on her four-poster bed and closed her eyes as instructed. She was about to enter the world of society. It was something to which she had never aspired. The bustle of preparations, the delight of the new dresses, of the amusing dancing lessons, had obscured the end to which they all pointed. Now it was upon her, this very evening. She would have to face this unknown world and suddenly she plunged into the depths. She couldn't. She knew so little of people, of customs. The thought of the formidable, disapproving dowagers, the cold, haughty gentlemen with their quizzing glasses raised so cruelly for inspection, the sneers of the girls of lofty families whose whole upbringing had been devoted to this very event, was demoralizing. How could she, Christina Kelway, face them all and hold up her head? There was no one to help her, to say something encouraging. Her father, so pleased at what he had arranged for her, Lady Lethbridge, so kind but taking her world for granted, Audrey, undoubtedly in the quakes, there was no one to understand and sympathize. No one on whom she could rely if anything went wrong.

As the words crossed her mind she saw a tanned, bony face and vivid blue eyes. If only Sidi were here, someone she would encounter, who would find something to laugh at with her and put a strong hand under her arm. She felt tears running down her cheeks and buried her face in her pillow. Sidi would have listened to her and nodded and understood and helped her put away her fears. The tears came faster. She *needed* him. Why hadn't he come? He had taken charge at Boulak, at Alexandria, he would always know what to do. She gave another sob. How could she get on in this new world alone?

She gave a gulp and the sound surprised her. She would have to. She pushed the tears away from her cheeks. She could, for her father's sake. She would hold up her head and face them all and try to put on an air of belonging, and rely on herself. But . . . she felt another tear and jumped from the bed. Red eyes would be no assistance in facing the beau monde. As she bathed her eyes she allowed herself to think a moment again on Sidi and wonder where he was and what kind of man he was now and told herself she might never see him again and she had best bury him once more at the bottom of her mind.

Though Lady Spofford's ball might be considered to be a trifle early, for it was the first of the season, it was evident from the procession of coaches that many had made a push to attend. Here was her second test, Chris knew, as she went up step by step the marble staircase to the ballroom. But she had passed the first test. She knew her ball gown was *right,* a pale primrose with a trim of artificial pearls and a gauze overskirt of slightly darker shade, which looked well beside Audrey's blue. But she had never seen such an assemblage of fashion and elegance as that mounting with her, and, dismayed, looked to Audrey. The fright and amazement on the pink and white face brought her a quick feeling of superiority—for she was sure she was not showing her feelings—and she reached and squeezed the somewhat damp hand beside hers. It was something of a relief to have to wait in line to be presented, for it gave her a chance to take three deep breaths and remember to hold up her head.

But she almost gasped at sight of the ballroom. Deep purple draperies at long windows alternated with pale yellow panels holding wide sconces and long mirrors; the chairs and scattered small sofas shared the same color scheme. A cleared space showed there would be

77

dancing. Then she was curtsying, without mishap, to an imposing lady in purple taffeta and an even more imposing gentleman in scarlet who were greeting each guest with a slight air of complacency.

"They can tell already that the affair will be a success," Lady Lethbridge whispered as she steered them toward a sofa where four gentlemen were conversing. "You young people go and dance. You may waltz here but not until I tell you at Almack's, and you may dance more than twice with a gentleman if that should prove to be necessary, which I doubt. Remember to return to me after each dance. Now, enjoy yourselves," and she smiled at them happily.

Chris blessed Aunt Letty, as she must think of her, for her forethought about the dancing lessons and the escorts. Sir Gavin maintained a flow of light talk with little suggestions about the figures which he interspersed whenever she hesitated and at the end said she was doing him credit and asked for the first waltz. Mr. Bowman was also unobtrusively helpful during the next dance and she gained in assurance. By the time she had enjoyed a rather stately dance with her father, which gave them a chance to compliment each other on their appearance, and promenaded briefly with Lord Lethbridge, Chris began to feel the new life might prove enjoyable at times.

There was a cluster around Lady Lethbridge when they returned, a gray-haired dowager in puce and two gentlemen. "Lady Allonbury has brought two who wish to meet you, my dears," Lady Lethbridge said after the introduction.

"Indeed, yes," gushed that lady. "You have been in some distant spot, I hear, Miss Kelway, so I simply had to make known to you Lord Ashburn, who was in Egypt a while ago and talks about it in the most enchanting fashion, and the Comte de Oudenard, who has just escaped from that horrid Napoleon and come to join our French group. And Miss Cadwell, who is from Sussex, will be just as charmed, I know." Looking highly satisfied by a good deed well done, she hurried away down the room.

Chris gave the dip demanded by the occasion and looked at the two gentlemen. Lord Ashburn was striking, with tossed dark hair and black eyes, but her first thought was his nose and chin were too prominent. She turned her gaze on the Comte and only by a strong effort of will did she refrain from gasping. The man was the one who had been Captain Oudenard on the banks of the Nile. There was the small moustache, the bright dark eyes in the round face; the hair beneath the officer's cap had been black also. He was looking at her and Audrey with appreciation and not a flicker of recognition. She kept her eyes blank and smiled and accepted Lord Ashburn's arm for the next dance.

He was a good dancer, so she had to concentrate a little on the figures. But the lady was supposed to entertain the gentleman or at least lead him to talk himself. So as soon as she felt she could follow the dance without trouble and they came together for a few moments she began, "You have had exciting travels, my lord?"

"Any travel can become an adventure, Miss Kelway," he drawled, "but pray do not ask me to recount some. That is the ordinary chatter of young ladies on the dance floor and you are not the ordinary type so I expect better things of you."

"Then I certainly will not quiz you," she answered with spirit, quite sure that was a compliment of sorts, which brought a very slight smile to the rather small mouth. "You undoubtedly realize I am quite green, so pray tell me something of these impressive people we are passing and repassing."

"That is a subject much more to my liking," he approved. "Lady Southwell, over there, the one in the unpleasant pink gown, having done her duty by her lord and produced three children, two boys, is now in town endeavoring to fill her quiver with ciscebos and having a little difficulty. You see, she and Mrs. Hemlin, that extravagantly orange brunette who is even more beautiful, are rivals for the same gentlemen. The betting is about even, so far."

Chris blinked. That was not what she had expected to hear but it had its own fascination. "Yes," she breathed encouragingly.

"The stout young man with the embroidered blue vest is the possessor of a large fortune, mills I believe, there are better connections on his mother's side; he is on the hunt for a girl with a good title, and will probably succeed." He paused and bowed to a willowy blonde who gave him a warm yet secretive smile. "Lady Whitehorn," he said in a different voice. "One of the loveliest of ladies and the cause, I may tell you, of my absenting myself from London for nearly a year."

"Why was that, sir?"

"She refused my offer and also that of an acquaintance, so we left England together to seek distraction. Our fortunes were not large enough for her or her parents. But she married an elderly fortune and now she looks with favor on old friends who are younger." He had returned to his weary drawl but gave a vigorous whirl.

"Do you know all the people here?" Chris asked in some awe. He was sounding as if he did.

"Many," he allowed with satisfaction, "and most of the *on dits* and *crim. cons.*, particularly since my return from my travels and the little talks I give, on request, about the lands I have visited and particularly Egypt. That is only to entertain at small parties, you understand. But now we seem to be contemplating an attack on that country my observations are quite in demand and of course I encounter people in the government who are anxious to inform themselves as easily as possible."

"I hope I may hear a talk," she ventured. She would have liked to exchange views, but it was evident he kept his for public display only.

"That might be possible someday," he allowed graciously as the dance ended and he returned her to Lady Lethbridge, and Audrey and the Comte. Audrey's prettiness was enhanced by a glow of pleasure as the Comte thanked her. He turned to Chris and begged for the next dance. Walking beside him to the floor she was wondering if she should speak of the earlier encounter and decided swiftly against it. He might be a relative of that other man, which would account for the resemblance. Also Lady Lethbridge had warned her not to mention Egypt, for it did not do for a girl to be knowledgeable about anything but fashions and gossip and acquaintances and nothing frightened away gentlemen so unerringly as a display of information they did not share. So she turned to France as a safe topic.

The Comte was happy to talk about that, or any aspect of his military experiences. He had joined the army being raised by the First Consul to invade Italy and, later, Egypt. Those experiences had been enlightening for a young man. His English was excellent, due, he claimed, to an English governess in his family. He had only been in England for three weeks, he explained, and was delighted with the country, the people, even most of his fellow refugees. "They were so warm, so hospitable," he exclaimed. "They took such pains I should find the right dress, acquire the dancing." He had come with letters to several of the French noblemen already established in and around London and through one had met Lady Spofford only four days ago. "And, *me voilà*," he beamed, "a stranger, yet welcomed in the highest circles and dancing with delicious young ladies. It is *formidable*. Your friend, Miss Cadwell, is ravishing. She says she is from the country?"

That did not mean she was countrified, Chris explained quickly. Her father's estate was in the country, yes, but his wife was a sister of Lord Lethbridge and that was how Audrey came to be visiting.

"Ah, yes." He looked thoughtful for a moment. "You are so kind to explain. I may hope to encounter you and Miss Cadwell throughout this season? I hope it will be of a great frequency," he added gallantly.

Sir Gavin was waiting to claim his waltz and Chris enjoyed the sensation of being almost popular. He would be knowledgeable about people, so she asked him cautiously about one or two of the handsome and bejeweled ladies. His comments were bright but without malice, and she ventured to ask what he knew of Lord Ashburn and the Comte.

"Pray make allowance for me, Miss Kelway. I was admitted to these ranks only two years ago and that is not one thirtieth of the time necessary to learn about the members of society. I only know the bits I have heard." He wheeled her gracefully to avoid a threatening couple who were making heavy weather of the dance. "Lord Ashburn, I gather, cuts something of a swath, a near-Corinthian. His fortune is unknown but he seems to feel no shortage of the necessary. His temper is uncertain."

"He looks as if he had one," Chris observed, "and is well satisfied with himself."

"Always. Except when Lady Whitehorn, she was something else then, refused both his offer and Lord Falkner's and they flung themselves off to travel."

"He would. And the Comte?"

"Oh, he is an unknown quantity, just arrived, you see. But his address is affable and he will be popular. There is nothing like a slight accent to engage a lady's appreciation."

"Not mine," Chris told him firmly and they laughed together and remarked how well they danced, she bestowing the credit on his teaching and he insisting it was her own lightness, and she thought what an engaging young man he was.

As they reached Lady Lethbridge once more an older man, taller, with a rather long face, halted beside them. "Lady Lethbridge has given me permission to dance with Miss Kelway," he began, "so be a good chap and introduce me, for she is engaged in a flirtation with some distinguished earl and will not care to be interrupted."

To her surprise and pleasure Chris saw that the earl was her father, who was bantering with Aunt Letty but quickly looked up to encounter her serious gray eyes above an appreciative smile.

"All right, if I have to," Sir Gavin said with an air of mock reluctance. "Miss Kelway, may I present my old friend and sometimes mentor, when necessary, Sir Alec Frayfield?"

Chris dipped, Sir Alec bowed and offered his arm. "Well done, Gavin, and my thanks. Miss Kelway, you will be most kind if you will allow me this dance." And he moved her away.

Though not so sprightly as Sir Gavin, he had an easy flow of question and comment and a warmth in his eyes she found gratifying. "I have been watching you, ma'am," he soon confessed, "and it was evident you were the one girl in the room I wished to meet. That desire was enhanced when Lady Lethbridge confided in me a secret I must not reveal."

Chris gave him a surprised glance as the figure separated them. She had no secrets, or, she amended, none that Aunt Letty could know. "If it is my secret you can reveal it to me," she pointed out roguishly as they came together again.

"It would take far more time to do it justice than we are permitted by this—exercise," he told her solemnly. "May I be permitted to call, to take you driving tomorrow afternoon?"

No one else had requested that particular pleasure. "Oh, please do," she burst out with improper warmth.

"Splendid," he said with equal warmth.

Then, as the dance ended, "You cannot as a gentleman leave me in suspense for all those hours," she pointed out.

"You have been warned against revealing it, also. That puts me at an advantage of which I shall make the most," he said quite seriously.

"Oh, go *on*." She would have liked to slap the arm on which her hand rested so decorously.

"I am reluctant, but I see I must. It is that you have spent several months recently in Egypt. I envy you."

"How nice you are interested," she exclaimed.

"I look forward to hearing of it on our drive."

She positively glowed. "I will be most happy to tell you ..."

"May I come at four? I must now receive permission from Lady Lethbridge. Thank you for the most delightful dance of the evening. Until tomorrow, then ..."

Left by herself for a moment, Chris openly watched the nearby groups of elegant people. Though not all the men were handsome nor all the ladies lovely, as had been her first impression, they all at least had an air of assurance about them that she wondered if she could ever achieve. Her glance passed over the adjacent group and suddenly, beyond them, she was gazing into two very blue eyes. She stared, gasped, "Sidi," and
84

smiled widely. The blue eyes held hers for one second and then looked away with no sign of recognition. She gasped again. Only one man had such eyes in a lean face. How *could* he cut her? Her first instinct was to push her way to him and demand what he meant by ignoring her, but then she knew that would be not only improper but unwise. And, there came a lowering thought, perhaps he had not recognized her . . . or perhaps did not wish to.

"Did you see someone you know?" Lord Ashburn drawled at her side. "You were smiling so . . ."

"I was smiling with pleasure at the sight of so many distinguished persons," Chris countered with what she felt was admirable self-possession. "I am green to all this, you remember."

"You will not be for long," he murmured as he looked her up and down in a fashion she felt vaguely offensive. "May I have the pleasure of this dance?" As he bowed, very slightly, he brushed Sir Alec, who was backing away. Both men murmured some apology and Chris, glancing back, saw Sir Alec was watching them.

"Unusual chap," remarked Lord Ashburn, though he had not seemed to notice the turn of her head. "Bookish. Was in the army, now in the Foreign Office."

"And what do you do, sir?" she asked as they faced and joined hands for the first figure. She must put those eyes from her mind.

"What I wish. I prefer to expend my energies on my own interests and pleasures," he drawled as they turned. As she tripped around the next gentleman she noticed that a dimpled, laughing Audrey was dancing again with the Comte. She must think of a topic of conversation and the Comte reminded her.

"And one of those interests you said is travel?" she asked in a short promenade.

"Indeed. Before the French spread the war around

I had visited much of the Continent. Then I took to more distant lands, Greece, Turkey, North Africa. One can travel in adequate comfort if one insists and has sufficient funds to support the insistence." The memories must have gratified him, for the narrow mouth curved into a somewhat larger smile than usual. "In fact, travel can be very remunerative if things are managed with a certain skill. I must admit I am regarded as something of an expert on Turkey and Egypt."

"But..." Christina began, though with no clear thought.

"You will perhaps be able to attend one of my little talks sometime, Miss Kelway, and so learn more." He was kind and condescending. "It is a pleasure to find a young lady who wishes to be instructed," he added graciously and bowed and left her.

"You did not mention Egypt to him, my love?" Lady Lethbridge asked anxiously. "He has made himself quite an authority on Egypt, you must know, in fact, the only one, I believe. Don't breathe a word. Though I did tell dear Sir Alec, but he is quite a different sort of man."

"Yes, I can see that," Chris agreed absently. "Is my father still here?" Perhaps he had seen Sidi, recognized, even spoken to him.

"Oh, no, he and Freddy left for the club after doing the proper things. I wish they had stayed a little longer but they agreed, quite naughtily, there were too many unmanageable cows waiting for partners and fled. We must go soon, now, ourselves."

During the last dance with Mr. Bowman Chris allowed herself to look around the room in quest of a figure, taller than most, with a close-cropped tawny head and blue eyes. She had no success and so concerned herself with entertaining this agreeable young man.

All the way home in the coach, while Audrey entertained Lady Lethbridge with her exicted chatter, Chris wondered about that glimpse. Perhaps she had been mistaken, as she probably was about the Comte. How could the starving ex-slave of some sherif on the Nile come to appear at a fashionable ball? English as he was, and well born as her father believed, how could he have effected this transformation? She had to find out, see him again, yes, ask him to return the two gold figures, if he still had them. But who would know him? How could she ask about a man of whom she only could say that he was tall and thin with short hair and blue eyes? She couldn't... She must not evince that interest, lay herself open to speculations about her past, her motives. No, it would be shaming. She would have to wait. But at least she knew she had passed the second test of the season and could feel she need not concern herself about her ability to make her way.

Once, when Audrey paused for breath, Lady Lethbridge asked Chris how she had enjoyed the evening and what she thought of the men she had encountered.

"It was such a glittering ball I was vastly impressed. I enjoyed myself immensely. The men seemed pleasant," she allowed guardedly.

"Which of them did you prefer? I trust it is Sir Alec, since he calls tomorrow."

"He is driving me in the park. Yes, I believe he is the most appealing," Chris said with some enthusiasm.

The drive in the park proved an event of interest and pleasure. Sir Alec and his dark green phaeton matched each other in their quiet elegance. The afternoon was sunny. The turnouts varied from an old-fashioned landaulet full of gaping schoolgirls to high-perch phaetons with dashing ladies and gentlemen gaily greeting friends as their shining horses pranced. The fascination of the colorful parade made it difficult for Chris to school her countenance to a semblance of passivity. On occasion she suffered a relapse and poked the arm beside her to demand who was some particularly lovely female with two gentlemen riding beside the curricle she graced, or two black-swathed dowagers who apparently ignored everything and everyone. Entertained by her queries and exclamations, Sir Alec did his best to satisfy her curiosity and usually had some bright anecdote to recount.

She felt she could not become surfeited by the sights, but politely agreed a change would be welcome when he turned into a side street and another that led to what was almost a country road, where he slowed the horses to a walk and turned in his seat. "There, Miss Kelway, you have seen the park at its best. May I now claim my reward and ask you about Egypt?"

She examined his likable face and agreed wholeheartedly, for he seemed to have a genuine desire to hear of the country. "Of course, sir. But why are you so eager to hear?"

"Because it has long been my desire to travel. My father prevented that in my youth. Oh, he meant well and we are fond of each other. I am the only son, you see, and he was convinced that the dangers of foreign travel far outweighed any possible benefits."

"But you were in the army," she exclaimed.

"Indeed. After Oxford he ignored my pleadings and saw to it I joined what appeared a safely staid regiment and nearly fell into a despondency when we were ordered to India. When I returned safely and in good health from a period I had enjoyed, he firmly placed me in the Foreign Office. I had not the heart to cause him further distress for he was old and ill. He died a year ago. I have been in London for four years."

"You could go away now?"

"I have tried for leave to join the army or for a foreign post but am told I am needed here. But, one way or another, something will turn up whether or not Bonaparte is satisfied with his conquests. We all have a particular interest in Egypt now that our fleet, one of our fleets, will be sailing to take over that land."

"Why should we wish to do that?" Chris demanded. "Except along the Nile it is mostly sand, which is most unpleasant to walk in, and the cities are poor and not at all likable."

"It is because of the feeling we must oppose the French at every point. The Pasha, who, you know, is appointed by the Sublime Porte, the Sultan of Turkey, but is practically independent, is about to ally himself with the French. So we are involved with the Mamelukes, the beys, his opponents, who also wish to control the land."

"I think it is silly of us," Chris said with some heat. "Our ships cannot go up the Nile and soldiers carry too much weight to be able to march well in sand."

He gave her a thoughtful look. "We would be better off with you as an adviser than some we have. And the people?"

"Father says they are not at all reliable."

"Ah, yes, your father is Lord Ingram, who recently presented to the Society of Antiquaries his impressive copies of the wall paintings of a tomb he had found."

"Indeed he is. And I helped him, for I did the colorings."

"You have my admiration, for I hear they are remarkable. What a strange life it must have been. Were you ever frightened?"

That surprised her. "No, of course not. I was with

my father and he had a firman from the Pasha. But," she added, wrinkling her forehead with distaste, "once, I confess, I was aghast for a moment."

"Why was that?"

"It was at a double temple called Kom Ombo, high on the bank of the river, above Thebes and Edfu. Only one of the temples remains but there are rooms, like cells, all around the edges, or some of them, not in front, of course. We turned a corner at the back and here was a room, dark and deep. It was half filled with mummified crocodiles, all facing us, with their teeth gleaming white out of the blackness. I screamed, which I should not have, and jumped, and took a hard hold on my father's arm."

Sir Alec threw back his head and laughed. "No wonder. I take it you departed quickly. An abominable sight. Tell me of how you lived, without any other horrors, I trust."

All the way back to Cavendish Square they talked of Egypt. He asked such right questions and was so interested Chris spoke freely of the trials and pleasures. Whenever Sidi came into her mind she firmly put him out.

"There is a friend I must make known to you who is also returned from Egypt," he said once in a slight pause. "You would enjoy each other."

"It is not Lord Ashburn?"

"No. He and I are acquaintances only. I am aware he makes something of a parade of his knowledge of Egypt and other lands. You would do well to follow Lady Lethbridge's advice and withhold your own views. Do not tangle with him. He holds himself *the* authority and brooks no other opinions."

"He seems that kind of man, though he made himself pleasant when we danced," she added in all fairness, and then returned to a discussion of animals and how odd it was that that no camels appeared on the wall pictures of ancient days when they were omnipresent now.

At the house they agreed the drive had been of the greatest pleasure and she readily agreed to save him two dances at Almack's two nights hence.

It was there that she found the erstwhile Sidi. Lady Sefton had given laughing permission for Lady Lethbridge's two girls to waltz and Chris had been enjoying her first with Sir Alec. They had been discussing the disappointing decor of the rooms, quite too plain, she held, and he agreed solemnly and warned the refreshments would be even more simple and not very appetizing. One came to Almack's for other purposes than to gratify a fondness for elegance, he pointed out, for even more than elsewhere it was the people who should hold one's attention. True, many scorned the place, but more attended to see and be seen, and one never knew whom one might encounter.

The waltz ended. Partners saluted each other and began to stroll down the floor. Sir Alec gave a slight start. "I seem to have developed prescience, Miss Kelway. As I was saying, one never knows who will appear at Almack's. Here is my friend Falkner, who has not appeared for some time." He steered her around a dawdling group and they came up to a back clad in navy superfine as impeccably tailored as Sir Alec's own; Sir Alec touched the shoulder. "Kirby, my dear chap. Good to see you. May I present you to Miss Kelway? She has..." He caught himself and gave Chris a look of comical dismay. "...but recently come to London. Miss Kelway, Lord Falkner."

The tall figure turned. "Alec! Glad you are here. Miss Kelway, your most obedient." He raised his head from the modest bow and Chris found herself looking

91

straight into the blue eyes she had first seen beside the Nile. And there was not a flicker of recognition in them.

She remembered to make a slight dip and sought for something to say that would startle the man into awareness. But thoughts failed her and there was the man beside him to meet, she never did hear his name, and she could only try to make her own eyes expressionless as she gazed upward. He was not only not recognizing her, he was not evincing the slightest sign of interest.

"You two should have a talk someday," Sir Alec went on a little hurriedly. "I'll see to it."

"A pleasure I shall anticipate," murmured the quiet, unchanged voice without a shade of conviction. "And you, Alec, dinner tomorrow night? Splendid." He turned to the man beside him and Sir Alec removed her rather hastily.

"Almost gave you away there," he whispered mischievously. "Don't you think the ban on your adventures might be lifted for him?"

Chris was conscious her hand rested a little too heavily on the arm beneath it and hoped it might be attributed to the crush of people. That man. What did he mean by not knowing her? "Is there any particular reason why it should be?" she managed to ask coolly.

"Oh, Kirby isn't a gabster, he wouldn't reveal a secret. And, yes, there is a reason. About three years ago he went off on some travels after his offer had been declined by a certain lady. He stayed on in Egypt when his companion came home. Once he told me in confidence that he had been stricken by a strange malady, all very vague, and as a result lost bits of his memory. He's more withdrawn now, though not on the surface, for he seems to be dallying after Lady Ottilie Wisworth, that lively brunette by the window. I'd like to help him—thought if you talked of Egypt that might aid his memory. But only if you wish."

She looked at him limpidly. "Any friend of yours, sir, would always be a pleasure to encounter."

For a moment he was pleased, then chuckled. "Coming too strong, dear Miss Kelway, but some friends, yes, you might enjoy. But I'll manage to keep your secret, never fear."

Chapter Seven

There came a rout, at which Chris heard some complaints that the crush was too great for pleasure but which she and Audrey enjoyed immensely, and another ball. Audrey's popularity had increased with more men clamoring for her dances and both Lord Ashburn and the Comte de Oudenard greatly in evidence. This all, she confided, was just what her mother had desired and she herself derived satisfaction from her popularity.

"Not to cover it in fine linen," Sir Gavin said, as he and Chris revolved in a simple figure, "word has spread somehow that she is a considerable heiress. Attracts all, you know, and some hedgerow jacks among them. Do you think I should take it on myself to suggest to Lord Lethbridge he warn off some of the court cards? Not sure how up to snuff he is on such things."

"Yes, I think you should," Chris advised when she returned to him. "It is most likely he does not know the—the more impecunious gentlemen. I do not doubt he would wish to protect her."

"My thought. I'll see what I can do. Feel responsible for you girls, first friends and all that."

"That is comforting to know." Chris was touched. "I trust there will be no problems."

"I'll throw them into the river if there are," he promised. "Only sorry not yet able to be in the petticoat line myself, for you're the best girl I've known." They gazed at each other with great friendliness and understanding, and Chris wished, as she remembered she had once before, that she had had just such a brother. There had been no sight of Lord Falkner at any of the affairs.

The next day Sir Alec invited Lord and Lady Lethbridge and the girls to a performance at the Royal Italian Opera House in Haymarket, an invitation that sent Chris and Audrey into the alts. "I've persuaded Kirby to accompany us," he told Chris as they shared a sofa at tea. "It seems the singer will be Catalani in some Mozart work which he would like to hear. He will be the escort for Miss Cadwell, of course, and I hope Lady Lethbridge will permit me to take you all to a light supper afterward. But I'll turn him over to you at the intermission, for I believe you could become friends. May I not tell him your secret, Miss Kelway? He will guard it."

Chris thanked him gaily for the treat his invitation would bring them all, then added thoughtfully, "Perhaps it would be better if you left it to me to speak of Egypt. I could bring up the subject and watch how he responds and judge whether I should push the matter further or execute a strategic retreat."

"Wise as always," he approved. "I know I can trust you to treat him with kindness. He is very reticent, as

I once said, speaks seldom of himself, is adept at concealing his feelings. Even if nothing develops I will at least have succeeded in making you somewhat better acquainted."

Chris allowed that undoubtedly all his friends were delightful, and began to look forward more than ever to the opera.

After some thought she donned blue silk with slightly darker braid trim around sleeves and hem and down the front of the overskirt of the same material. Audrey had chosen a favorite bright rose with gauze overskirt and trim that was more elaborate. Lady Lethbridge approved both and said with complacency that there were no more tastefully dressed and attractive girls to be seen this season. That reassurance, no matter how often it was said, was sustaining to Chris, for she knew she was not a beauty and that her respectable prospects did not put her in the ranks of the heiresses and that she would have to make her friends on whatever qualities she might possess and trust a sufficient number of people would find her amusing and agreeable. Sir Alec gave every indication of genuine appreciation, which was also a sustaining thought, for he was obviously an attractive and intelligent man esteemed by a wide circle.

She and Audrey gazed with awe as they entered the vast amphitheater of the opera house and followed the Lethbridges and Sir Alec to the box in the second tier near the stage. Already the pit and the gallery were crowded and the noise from them and from the five rows of boxes was overwhelming. The two just looked at each other in amazement from time to time, since they could not have heard a word either had spoken. All of the ladies in the boxes were *en grande tenue* and the colors and jewels that filled the corridors and boxes were nearly as overwhelming as the noise. As they entered Sir Alec's box a lean figure rose, was introduced, and when cloaks were removed seated himself beside Audrey in the third set of seats.

"It is quite remarkable you secured such an admirable box, dear Sir Alec." Lady Lethbridge adjusted herself to the gilt chair. "There is hardly a duchess of note who is not here tonight. Ah, there is dear Sally Jersey," and she leaned on the edge to wave across the wide space to the laughing lady in effective green. In fact, everyone seemed to be waving to someone else and frequently, Chris came to believe, people waved just to show they were equally important and without any particular friend in view. She leaned forward also, marveling, questioning, and Sir Alec was as diverted by her enthusiasm as she was by the sights. For the most part the boxes fell silent when the curtains parted, but nothing could halt the bedlam from the pit and the gallery, and Chris wondered how those in the boxes high and toward the back could hear the singers. But almost instantly she was lost in the magic of the opera and the magnificent voices. It was *The Magic Flute* and she sat enthralled and silent with the others in the box.

There was a slight pause as the curtains closed and then the figures in the boxes began to stir and the waves of sound began to swell. "This is all too entertaining not to take advantage of everything, dear Sir Alec. What wonderful voice and presence she has. Now we are going to call on friends." Lady Lethbridge rose, smiled at her lord, and the two sailed from the box.

Sir Alec asked Audrey if she would care to promenade and she jumped up so quickly she had to laugh at herself. Chris was torn. She would have enjoyed strolling and marveling but here was her one chance to probe into the mystery, so she shook her head.

"You must entertain Miss Kelway," Sir Alec admonished as he left, "and do bring her out if she changes her mind."

"Would you not prefer ... ?" Lord Falkner asked, one hand on the back of the empty chair and looking faintly puzzled.

"Let us sit a few minutes," Chris offered. "It may be less crowded shortly."

He sat down again. "I find at times I do not care for these excessive masses of people, but, when you wish ... for it is a strange sight and Alec tells me you are new to London." His expression was noncommittal. In the navy and white of the proper evening dress he was a figure of unobtrusive elegance except, as she noticed again, that his hair was very short and curled all over his head instead of being long enough to furnish a fashionable forelock or some waves. He must have had it cut very very short, and now it fitted his face.

The three tactful openings she had devised vanished from her mind. A deep hurt combined with anger and outrage took over. "Sidi," she said, more forcibly than she had intended, "what do you mean by acting this way? You know perfectly well you remember."

There was no flicker on the politely expressionless face before her, no glint in the blue eyes. "Pray tell me, Miss Kelway, how I am acting and what I should remember."

The voice was so courteous it infuriated her further. "You remember, of course you remember, Clio's tomb, the storehouse, my father, copying the walls of the tomb, the boat downriver ..." She knew, and regretted, that her voice shook. There was no sign of recognition at the words.

"You are claiming that I should know these extraordinary objects you are listing?" he asked with polite incredulity.

"Of course I am. We saved you from the sherif. And you saved us at Alexandria."

"That would seem to even the score then, whatever had happened."

"No. There was so much . . ." She flung out her hands in despair. "You *must* recollect."

"I would be happy to oblige you, of course, Miss Kelway, but I have no idea what you are talking about." The last words were clipped and final.

She stared at him aghast. Only remote tolerance showed on that face. There was nothing to which she could appeal. She jumped to her feet. "Since you persist in claiming ignorance, my lord, let us go and promenade."

Little remained with her of the spectacle and the people she passed. It took a great effort of will to concentrate on the next act of the opera and blot out the tall, lying, abominable man behind her. She shook her head a little to Sir Alec and hoped he understood that to mean she had had no success with his friend, and then was very vivacious at the elegant supper he had ordered for his guests. Amid her thanks he managed to suggest a drive the next afternoon.

But as her head went down on the pillow she began to cry. It was disappointment, she told herself, at not finding the friend she had expected. No. She sobbed and sat up. It was fury that Sidi should behave this way. Deny her, her father, all they had done for him! Not even acknowledgment! He might have forgotten what had happened to him before he was struck on the head but he couldn't forget the weeks he had spent with them. The tears dried unnoticed. What was his reason for denying them? Perhaps she'd never know, which was infuriating also. Her father had not encountered him or it would have been mentioned, probably their paths never crossed. And they might not recognize each other, no beards. But she had had no difficulty. Her glance fell on her chest in the corner. Laughter bubbled up without warning inside her. Suppose she should produce that license ... tell that man she wished to be proclaimed as Lady Falkner ... ushered into society on his arm ... What a joke it would be! And how that aloof face would be confounded! He'd have to acknowledge her. She laughed some more and shook her head. No, she could never use it. Her father must have forgotten all that fever-ridden night and so had this Falkner. But it was an amusing thought, and she went to sleep smiling.

For the drive with Sir Alec she wore a daffodil-yellow sarsenet trimmed with blue braid and a matching hat with a plume. She had left behind the parasol Audrey had suggested as she felt she did not yet manage it with sufficient dexterity to keep it from interfering with her view of the sights around her. She knew she must allow the gentleman to give his undivided attention to driving in the crowded streets, but as soon as they turned into the park she asked brightly if he had seen his friend Lord Falkner.

The well-bred face was calm but a faint line appeared between the straight brows. "Only briefly, at Wattier's. We spoke of nothing of interest except his enjoyment of the opera, the company I provided, and the Catalani's singing. But, enlighten me. You shook your head, you had no success with him on the subject of Egypt?"

"Alas, no." Chris shook her head again and then had to be sure her bonnet was still in place. "I mentioned Egypt, gently, of course. He denied any knowledge, in spite of what you told me, so I did not proceed further." That was shading the truth, but permissible, she felt.

"I do not understand." He frowned. "Of course Kirby

has always been infernally closemouthed about himself and his affairs, just like his father, family trait. Ashburn reported on his return that they reached Cairo and Kirby felt not quite the thing and decided to linger so they separated, after a very successful journey. Kirby just said he had found Egypt interesting, persuasive was the word he used, so he remained longer than he originally intended."

"Some find strange lands, antiquities, beguiling," Chris offered.

"If they have the right interests. I heard your father has brought back some extraordinary copies of wall paintings from a tomb."

"They're beautiful." Pride was in her voice. "And I did the colorings, as I think I told you."

Instead of following that lead he frowned again. "I also heard that Ashburn has taken offense at someone else being acclaimed as knowledgeable in his field."

"But Egypt is a vast land and there is so much of the past there many authorities will be needed in many fields. No one man could know it all."

"Perhaps it was only passing gossip. But Ashburn has set himself up as the one authority and there was a rumor someone in the war department talked of hiring him for a fat fee to assist in the coming invasion. Probably nothing will come of any of this," he added comfortably.

Hoping the same, Chris glanced back at the passing vehicles. "Here are Audrey and the Comte," she exclaimed and waved as much as good form allowed.

"Do you think Miss Cadwell is developing a *tendre* for any of the gentlemen who pursue her?" Sir Alec asked as they passed.

Conscience-stricken, Chris shook her head. She should have watched, listened more to what Audrey confided at such length. It was her duty to maintain some attention, for the girl was even more green than she was and a trusting child. "I do not think so," she hesitated. "She holds Viscount Rundle and Mr. Camberly the best of companions. But she finds Lord Ashburn and the Comte the most fascinating, both being of types she has not encountered."

"Inevitable, I am afraid."

"There is a childhood friend in Sussex she once said she would prefer to wed, but I do not know if he is now in her thoughts."

"There is no way of suggesting he come to London for a visit, I suppose," Sir Alec said thoughtfully. "She is innocent and wealthy, an unfortunate combination. I doubt if she would ever acquire sufficient town bronze for her own sake. She would be happier in Sussex."

"I have had the same thought. But I can hardly write an unknown man to come rescue his lady love."

"Difficult," he agreed amusedly. "I daresay all will be well. Now, I am wondering if I may be very daring and escort a party to Astley's Amphitheatre."

Chris nearly bounced in her seat with anticipation. "That is a famous notion. Indeed you may. I have heard of the marvelous riding there." And she resolved as she spoke to give Audrey more of her attention.

Apparently Audrey had felt no lack of concern, for the next afternoon she drew Chris into her room and shut the door. "I must consult with you, dear Chris," she began, "for I am not certain what course I should pursue."

"Have you heard again from your Jim?" It might be as well to remind the girl of her first gallant.

Audrey tossed her head. "A few days ago. But all he does is complain that I do not write him often and when I do it is of balls and gala affairs about which he can hardly share my emotions. No, this is much more important."

Chris sat down on the bed and folded her hands. "Tell me."

Audrey plumped down beside her and gave her a look compounded of shyness and mulishness. "It is Lord Ashburn. I find him the most elegant of gentlemen and, I confess, his attentions are quite exhilarating."

"He is certainly a man of the world," Chris agreed coolly, but her coolness was not noticed.

"Oh, yes, you put it so well. Last night, at the concert, he asked me to permit him to take me for a drive to a cottage he owns out in Islington. He says it is modest, just a place where he can retreat when he becomes weary of people and the exertions demanded of him. He would like my opinion of its decorations. He would take me in his curricle for tea and we would be back well before dinner."

Chris started to protest, but halted. It would never do to set up Audrey's back, so she turned stubborn, as could happen with anyone. "Did he mention who else would be of the party?"

A started look came over the glowing face. "Oh, no, he mentioned no one else. It is *my* opinion he wishes."

"How very flattering. But," and she made her voice a little perplexed, "do you really think it quite the thing to go alone?"

A faint cloud descended and the full underlip pushed forward. "You know more of society than do I, which is why I asked you. I can see no harm in it. But sometimes Aunt Letty is as strict as Mother, and they have so many rigid rules of behavior here. I was not entirely convinced I should go."

"What did you tell him?"

"That I would have to see—though he promised no one could object to any degree."

"But in your own heart you did..."

"I suppose so. What do you think? I would *so* like to go."

"I can see ... but I am quite sure it is not at all the thing for a young lady of your standing to undertake a visit to a gentleman's house, however modest, alone." Chris was feeling her way along the problem but there was really only one thing she could do, though she found it distasteful. "A delightful expedition, no doubt. But would you not enjoy more company?" A slight look of doubt was turned to her. "In truth, I would enjoy seeing Islington. Of course my opinion of the cottage would not be asked, but suppose you told Lord Ashburn you would be happy to drive there if he could accommodate me and some other gentleman?"

"We could go in his phaeton and I could sit in front with him and he could say all the agreeable things he somehow finds to tell me." Audrey clapped her hands. "That would be perfect. No one could question the propriety if there were four." She threw her arms around Chris. "I knew you could tell me what was best. I do so enjoy his company I was loath to miss an opportunity to be with him for more than a dance or a supper. He may set the afternoon?"

Chris let out a long breath when she returned to her room. Again she wished a few of the other gentlemen who had entered Audrey's orbit had made an equal impression. But his extra years and experience had given Lord Ashburn a suavity and assurance younger men inevitably lacked. And whoever might be the other man he brought she could endure him for an afternoon.

In a tan gown and bonnet she now found less appealing than when she had purchased it, she approached the waiting phaeton and the man standing beside it, and knew that for one moment shock and distaste showed on her face. An impassive Lord Falkner was holding out his hand to assist her to mount to the back seat. She would have liked to run back to the house but of course could not behave in such a ragbag fashion. She sat down, folded her hands over her reticule, and regarded them fixedly as weight lowered the end of the seat.

"I take it we are both surprised at our companion for this drive," Lord Falkner observed as the phaeton moved forward.

"Quite right, sir," she murmured, surveyed all the things that came to mind to say, and said nothing.

"Since we cannot escape our fate, then let us find some topics of mutual interest to pass the hours ahead." He was talking easily, usurping the role of the lady in such a case, but Chris felt no resentment, for he was obviously more socially adroit than she. "Alec said you were new come to London. We can compare impressions, for I only recently returned from a considerable absence and can view the place as practically a stranger."

London seemed a safe topic . . . and at the moment she did not care for the place at all, which perhaps would shut him up. "I do not see its vaunted beauty, sir, and I dislike the dirt and the noise," she began, a little belligerently.

"Whoever said it was beautiful had windmills in his head," he allowed. At that moment a mail coach, horns blaring, a child on the roof screaming against the yells of his mother, rolled past. "And I certainly agree about the noise. But let me share some of the amenities I have found." He went on to mention what he had enjoyed in recent weeks and imperceptibly Chris found he was no longer Sidi but Lord Falkner making himself agreeable to a lady foisted on his attention and began to agree with him that the afternoon parade was a colorful sight and some of the music available quite uplifting. To her surprise she found herself enjoying his description of a disastrous boating expedition up the Thames and was inexplicably pleased when he laughed at her descriptions of the Bond Street dandies on the strut of a morning. She had found that she thought of him, which of course she preferred not to do but he did seem to intrude when her mind was not occupied, occasionally as Sidi but with growing frequency as Lord Falkner. He was entirely the urbane gentleman as they agreed on the pleasures and pains of the opera and of Almack's. His face lighted during their banter, but became impenetrable again when the ride ended.

Lord Ashburn's cottage was on the London side of Islington. This was fortunate, he told them, turning in his seat, because it saved him the ennui of driving through the village with its streets so crowded they were often blocked entirely. If it had not been for the burden of such an effort he would have shown them the famous inn, the Angel, and the Great North Road, but they could be saved for another visit. The cottage, set a little back from the road, was a small Tudor-imitation dwelling in white plaster and black timbers, with two rooms below and two above, as the girls discovered when they mounted the steep stairs to wash the dust from their faces. Each bedroom was tidy and looked unused. The living room was equally tidy and comfortably furnished and decorated with sporting prints. Chris would have wagered the place was rented, for there was nothing in it that spoke of Ashburn.

Audrey insisted on seeing the kitchen, which was spacious, with a large fireplace at the far end and a pump by the rear door. At one side of the fireplace was a four-foot-high mound of brick, partly covered with plaster.

"What new invention is that, sir?" Audrey asked playfully. "I am convinced you add inventing to your other skills."

Lord Ashburn waved one white hand. "Merely a contrivance for the experiments with which I occasionally amuse myself, but no inventions, ma'am," he told her lightly, and pointed to some plates of delftware on the mantel for her to admire.

Since it was too chill to take tea in the garden it was brought to the living room by a cheerful country woman and abounded in thick creams and scones and tarts and eggs so fresh their host said he could still hear them cackling, which sent Audrey into whoops. When consulted, she said the decorations would be improved only by bright red curtains at·the windows, for they would be more cheerful. The suggestion was lauded by an appreciative Lord Ashburn, who came over much too thick and rare, Chris felt, and even more so when, awestruck, he agreed the name should properly be Rose Cottage. He entertained them with lively tales of adventures of his own and friends, none in Egypt, and it all passed with surprising speed. And they were back at Cavendish Square well before seven.

"Lord Ashburn is such a remarkable man," Audrey proclaimed at dinner, "he could keep anyone entertained for a lifetime. There cannot be another man like him." Her description of the pleasures of the afternoon were so enthusiastic Chris wondered if they had really been together.

The afternoon had brought her new uncertainties. During the past weeks she had recognized that the memories of Egypt had retreated into the background, something apart from the rest of her life. If she summoned up a picture it was vivid, Clio's tomb, the Nile in moonlight, the towering pillars at Karnak with their feet in sand and squalor, but entirely separate from

London. And now she was finding that the man Sidi had been displaced by the urbane Lord Falkner. But she felt that the Lord Falkner of the afternoon she could come to like in spite of his unaccountable denial of knowing her, and the unsolved mysteries.

Chapter Eight

Lord Ingram dined at Cavendish Square that evening. When the gentlemen had had their port and joined the ladies Chris slipped over to sit beside her father and tuck her hand into his. He pressed it, gave her his affectionate smile, and looked back at Lord Lethbridge. Chris knew that some dowagers would hold such a display of affection to a father improper, even at home, but her father had never discouraged such expressions, and of course she did not do it in public.

"It distresses me to continue with this unpleasant subject, Freddy," he was saying, "but I do not understand how this hesitation, this inquiry, has come about. Lord Frampton has been most enthusiastic."

"Neither do I, dear chap. Apparently Lord Sisley, he's in the war department, has taken up Ashburn's cause—their grandmothers were cousins—and is trying to push the matter. Ashburn, as we have all heard, will tolerate no other authority on Egypt. It is said he makes a pretty penny from his discourses on that land not only to people such as we but to merchants, businessmen. Not at all the thing, some hold. There is even the rumor the government is considering making him an official adviser to the army."

Lord Ingram rubbed his forehead with his free hand. "I do not perceive why those activities should make him hostile to my reproductions."

"A threat of another expert," Lord Lethbridge said airily, "and an impressive one."

"Is that horrid man making trouble for you, Father?" Chris would put nothing past Lord Ashburn.

"I am convinced it will come to nothing," Lord Lethbridge continued. "A screen of smoke, for some purpose of his own."

"All the same," and Lord Ingram moved uneasily, "I could wish you did not have to go down to Portsmouth to look at the troops. You are more expert than I in dealing with anything unexpected or official."

"It will come to nothing, old boy. We'll go to the club and forget it." They departed, still talking, leaving Chris vaguely troubled.

She was sufficiently troubled to ask Sir Alec, on a drive to Richmond for tea at the Bear and Staff, if he knew anyone at all who was involved with the Society of Antiquaries, for she felt the shadow of a cloud, however unknowable that cloud might be, hanging over her father. He said he did not have that pleasure. "Not in my line," was his final comment. Chris felt there was no one else she could consult, and a faint worry remained.

The morning after a grumbling Lord Lethbridge had departed for Portsmouth, where fleet and army were assembling, Lord Ingram appeared and took Christina into the library. It was a rather dark room anyway and as she sat down she feared it would be darker in a few minutes.

Her father began to pace up and down, running a

hand through his thick gray hair and looking at her with distress in his hazel eyes. "Perhaps I should not be bothering you, my dear. But you were my partner on our expedition and I have always had respect for your intelligence and your good sense. I doubt if anyone can help me. I do not expect that, now Freddy is gone, but I do want you to know what has occurred."

"Yes, Father." She sat very still, hands folded, and watched his face. "It sometimes is a help to share a problem."

"Precisely." That seemed to make it easier for him to talk. He sat down in the other armchair across from the fireplace. "What has happened, Chris, is that Lord Ashburn's inquiries and conjectures have resulted in something more unpleasant. I have been summoned to appear before some sort of governing board of the Society of Antiquaries and answer the charge that I have endeavored to foist off on them a series of drawings and paintings that are false and shed doubt on my ever having been in Egypt."

"Father!" Shock brought her up even straighter. "That is ridiculous, monstrous!"

"Of course." He gave her a bleak smile. "Some of the many words I have been using. But it is true."

"Tell me about it."

"Indeed, I'll be glad to set it out plainly." He stopped, shook his head, and resumed quietly. "It seems Lord Ashburn has sent a letter to Lord Frampton stating that the rolls of pictures which I, under the auspices of Lord Lethbridge, presented to the Society of Antiquaries are fakes and forgeries. He says they differ to such a marked degree from the rolls he brought over himself a year ago that there can only be doubt if I was ever in tombs and temples of Egypt. He does not wish the learned Society to be hoodwinked and demands that my contribution be denounced and removed from the hands of the scholars, from the Society and all others who might see them."

"But how can he do that? They will pay him no heed..."

"He chose a good time, with Freddy away, you see. Lord Frampton, as president, must investigate the charges and I have no one to speak for me. And Ashburn has enlisted Lord Sisley on his side, who has denounced me in extravagant terms as an impostor."

"Father! This is impossible, outrageous, wicked." Chris jumped from her chair, and seeing a book on the table picked it up and hurled it to a corner of the room. "Wish I could do that to him."

"My dear—the binding—though I appreciate your feeling. I confess my first thought was to go in search of a horsewhip. But we must not allow our outraged emotions to supersede our judgments."

Chris went for the book and replaced it, forgetting to note if the binding had been damaged. "We must do something."

He spread his hands. "But what, my dear? Freddy is the only man I know who could speak for me. Lord Frampton, in a courteous note, said I would be asked to produce proof that I had been in Egypt, as I have claimed, and that my reproductions of the pictures and hieroglyphics have truly been copied from some temple or tomb and are accurate. How can I produce proof?"

That his voice held a hopeless note showed how deeply he had been struck by this attack on his integrity.

Chris paced to the window. "Are there no other reproductions in London that could be examined?"

Again he shook his head. "I have heard of none. Freddy might have known."

She came back from the window, which only showed

the opposite wall of the mews. "When and where is this meeting?"

"Tomorrow evening," her father sighed. "Tomorrow evening at nine. At Somerset House in the Strand. And with not only Lord Frampton but the board of governors. It is a most eminent organization, you know, for it was formed in 1717 and later was given a charter by George the Second and then these rooms in 1780. Normally, it is an honor to appear there . . ." and his voice trailed away.

"Is there not anyone you could consult, who would accompany you?" He must not sink into a melancholy state.

"I can think of no one. I have spoken of our travels only casually, for few are interested. What I said in conversation would not be held proof."

"No, I can see that." She frowned and sat down again. "But how about the British Museum? There might be some reproductions there."

He brightened. "An excellent notion, my dear. I'll go to Montagu House this afternoon, after lunch has softened whomever I may consult." He straightened and rose. "See, you do have good ideas. And I feel better for having told you."

"And I am going to that meeting with you," she said firmly.

"You will not be permitted, as females are not allowed at such august gatherings."

"We will see about that," she announced grandly. "You will take me in a hackney."

To her surprise the old twinkle came into his eyes. "I will that, my dear, though I am loath to have you witness what may be a most uncomfortable encounter. I confess I would prefer Freddy, but failing him I will be happy to bring my dear daughter." He stopped and kissed her forehead. "You are a brave, sensible child.

Now, not a word of this to anyone. I will return to-morrow morning and acquaint you with anything I have learned."

"And you will come to dinner tomorrow night," she smiled. She wished she could ask him for this night but knew she was committed to a small dinner given by a friend of Aunt Letty's.

He nodded and managed a smile and left her.

Feeling she would like to walk to ponder the problem, Chris considered the garden but decided it was too small to contain her agitation. Since the others had gone out, she could take Rose and walk around the square, and since Rose had learned to walk behind her she could think in peace. She would have to do something . . .

Rose confided she was pleased to get out in the air though Cook and Housekeeper had been discussing, while Cook made meringues, the situation of the Prince Regent and Mrs. Fitzherbert with such absorption they had forgotten Rose was listening. She hadn't understood all the words, she ended with a tentative note.

"I can't explain them to you now," Chris told her, as she started along the walk, thinking she probably would not know them herself, much less how to explain them. "And I have to think." Docilely Rose dropped behind her, though Chris thought she heard mutterings from time to time.

This cannot happen to dear Father, she told herself first, as she turned the corner. I must find something. He said, she concentrated on remembering, he needed witnesses and proof. A black landaulet, two black hats visible above the side, paced past, followed by a phaeton bearing two laughing couples. Chris thought, and snapped her fingers. Of course there was a witness to their stay in Egypt, and on the bank of the Nile. He had been Captain Oudenard then. Well, that might be possible, a sort of *nom de guerre*, but, on the other hand ... She opened her parasol and practiced twirling it. On the other hand ... And he had seen her father there at the storehouse, working at his table. She nodded. Word of a comte would carry much weight. But, and she stopped her twirling, he was a Frenchman. Sir Alec had once said, when speaking of a recent book on Egypt, that no one believed what a Frenchie said. She would need another witness and was pained by her own obtuseness. Of course there was another, and an English lord at that. The two should convince anyone, no matter how doubtful or hostile. They must be persuaded to come.

At the dainty Louis Seize escritoire in her room she thought hard, for the phrasing of both notes must be delicate but firm. To the Comte she wrote that Lord Ingram's reputation and veracity were being unscrupulously attacked before the Society of Antiquaries by Lord Ashburn (she had to say who it was) and it was being questioned that he had even been in Egypt. She was convinced that M. le Comte would recall an evening on the banks of the Nile above Luxor when he had come upon Lord Ingram in a stone building, near a tomb, at work at his table reproducing the wall paintings and drawings he had discovered. Would he not be good enough to attend this meeting, and give time and place, and testify to that encounter? She was convinced he would wish to see justice done and Lord Ingram cleared of this infamous attack. There was, of course, no mention that it was Captain Oudenard with a patrol who had appeared, but she believed the memory of both meetings would hang over the note and that the Comte would be unwilling to have it known that not so long ago he had been slave hunting in the service of the Pasha of Egypt.

For five minutes she sat composing notes in her head

to the second witness. What could she say in a note to one who had denied all knowledge of her and her father that would bring him to such a meeting? Nothing, she decided. She would have to see him, and the thought was daunting. In the end she merely asked him to come and call on her as soon as possible on a matter of the utmost importance. And wondered, as she dispatched a footman with both missives, how long she would have to wait and even if he would deign to come at all.

She took resolution and went down to the library. There was an hour and a half to luncheon. If he did not come in that time it might mean he would never. But he came in under an hour, not strolling into the room, but not hurrying.

"Miss Kelway. I have your note." He held it up. "You say something of utmost importance. In what manner may I serve you?" He was using the polite, cool tones of a gentleman responding to a lady he scarcely knew.

"It is indeed of the utmost importance," she said steadily, and gestured to the armchair opposite hers. "You are in a position to save the honor and integrity of a gentleman from false accusations." She had decided to keep it all as impersonal as possible, at least at first.

"Indeed?" The eyebrows rose. "May I ask how?"

"You may not wish to do so." She had to give him a way to retreat, but he only showed the same remote courtesy. She took a long breath and looked at him. "You may wish to continue to deny that you were with Lord Ingram and myself on the banks of the Nile near Luxor. But you said, when you left us on the ship at Alexandria, that you could never repay our kindnesses to you. You now have a chance."

Again the eyebrows rose above half-closed lids.

Speaking quietly she quickly told him of the infamous charge of Lord Ashburn and the coming meeting.

"And what is it you wish me to do?" he asked softly.

"Appear at the meeting as a witness for my father and tell those dodoes, I mean those eminent gentlemen, that you saw Lord Ingram for a—a period of time, copying meticulously the wall paintings and carvings from a tomb." There, she had said it.

"But what if I do not wish to lend myself to this tale you have recounted? Oh," one hand went up, "I do not doubt about the meeting you mention. But I do not care to play the part you assign me."

"But you must." By an effort she kept her voice even. "As an honorable gentleman you cannot let another be vilified, ruined by malice and envy."

His eyes were wider now, watching her. "You mistake me. I can."

"Oh," she exploded, and stopped. Drawing a quick, shuddering breath she said carefully, "I do not understand."

"It is simply that my own purposes, intentions, plans are more important to me than the downfall of any honorable gentleman. I will let nothing stand in my way." The level of his voice never shifted from polite reasonableness.

"Not even to redeem a promise you made?" she asked in bewilderment.

"Not even that, much as I regret the necessity."

"So." She pounced. "You do remember the tomb, everything. If you did not you would not regret."

He rose swiftly and walked to the window and stood there, a tall figure in a dark green morning coat and dove-gray pantaloons. "I should not have used that word," he admitted ruefully, "and remembered how quick you are." He returned to his chair. "Yes, Miss Kelway, I will admit to you, since we are alone and without witnesses, that I do indeed remember my stay in Egypt, my days with you and your father, and how

117

infinitely much I owe you both. But I am dealing with my future. There are things I must discover. And I would be hampered if it came out how much I do recall." He was watching her intently.

"Is that your final answer to my plea?" she asked.

"It is."

"Then," she gulped and drew up her reticule and from it removed the little white bag, opened it, and smoothed the folded paper she removed. "Then," she took another breath, "perhaps this marriage license will alter that answer."

"What?" He was on his feet again.

"Yes," and she found she could smile at him. "Our marriage license, from Boulak."

"It's a forgery."

"Oh, no one who examines it would so believe, sir, with all the signatures, and, and our names."

He strode to her, holding out his hand. "Let me see it," he ordered harshly.

She slid from her chair and backed away. "Since you are not an honorable man I do not trust you with it," she said and laughed in his face.

"Vixen. At least bring it closer."

She edged a little closer and held it out, grasping it firmly in both hands. He rubbed one hand across his forehead, bent to peer, and backed away. "You would not use it."

"Oh, but I would, sir. I would be reluctant, for the idea has even less appeal to me than it has to you. But if you do not come to this meeting and testify on behalf of Lord Ingram I will show this to Lady Lethbridge, who will know how to make the most of it and you, and my story."

"Would it be believed?" He pointed at the paper.

"Oh, yes, with the signatures. And my father would not take kindly to what might be considered an insult to his daughter—since you have so obviously forgotten your obligations to her." She had a satisfactory vision of the lively Lady Ottilie frustrated.

"Why has he not sought me out?" Curiosity rode on the calm voice.

"I think he has forgotten. He was very ill, you remember, in a fever, in pain, poisoned, drugged. But he has a very good memory, I assure you, when it is awakened."

"And no one knows of this—document—but the three of us?"

"Only we three," she affirmed, beginning to fold and stow the paper away while he watched.

"I could deny it," he began abruptly, then rubbed his forehead again. "No, by then it would all be out." Once more he walked away and returned. "Very well, Miss Kelway, the game is yours. I will come tomorrow evening, give me the direction again and time, and testify for Lord Ingram. In return, you will stow that paper safely away, and keep it secret from all. You must promise me."

Hand poised, Chris promised. There were so many things she wished to ask him—but now was not the time. She must hope another would present itself.

The next morning her father came to tell her he had had no success at Montagu House. The keeper had been interested and produced a few copies from Egypt but so crude and inaccurate they could be no use to anyone. So her excellent suggestion had come to nothing.

She told him of the note she had sent to M. le Comte and that she had found Sidi, who was a Lord Falkner, and who would come to the meeting. At first her father was horrified, but at length agreed he did need men to stand up for him.

"I could not reach you for consultation when the two

men came to my mind—and the only two at hand who saw us. So I just went ahead..."

"Taking all fences." He managed a smile. "You believe they will come? Tell me of Sidi, when you can. I am most interested. Amazing you found him. Now I must go and have lunch at the club with a friend of Oxford days and act as if nothing has happened."

"You will—and nothing truly will," she promised and kissed him twice. Whereupon she informed Lady Lethbridge she had taken the liberty of inviting her father to dinner as he was escorting her to a meeting that had to do with Egypt afterward, and removed that from her mind a little by a shopping expedition to Bond Street.

For the so important meeting Chris chose a cream-colored long-sleeved dinner dress trimmed with tiny ruffles of the same material and tiny gold and blue buttons down the front to her waist and a narrow band of blue holding a simple blue gauze overskirt. She felt her costume was serious and dignified and could not be faulted. As she was placing the blue band in her hair the word *proof* exploded in her mind. Her father had used that, one thing desired. She nodded at the mirror. She had proof, and went to borrow from Mrs. Pritchett a pale blue silk bag intended for knitting. She would take the proof, but produce it only if necessary...

At dinner, Lady Lethbridge, after one glance at two serious faces, began to banter Lord Ingram about the youth they had shared and his escapades and scandals they had known and kept the five in forgetful laughter until the trifle was finished. She told them to run along to their dull meeting, for the footman would have a hackney any minute. They were at the door when she stopped them abruptly. "That cloak is too pale, Christina love. Audrey, fetch my blue taffeta. I take it you will be meeting with gentlemen; they always have a weakness for a good blue."

"Most becoming," approved her father as they settled in the hackney, "and the dress, my dear, is just what it should be. I confess my spirits are better than they have been these past days. Wise woman, Letty. But now, tell me quickly, how you found the erstwhile Sidi, in case he should appear."

This Chris had planned. "We are introduced by Sir Alec Frayfield. We recognized each other, and have encountered each other two or three times since. It is my opinion he does not care to pursue the acquaintance, but I was sure I could appeal to his sense of justice, and his gratitude to you."

"I certainly trust you are right, and respect your enterprise. If he does not care for our company that is his privilege, but I liked him. I would never have ... but I must see him sometime, for I am in debt to him for our passage money. Perhaps he will be willing to dine with me one night, after, after all this is over.... Now, forward to confound the enemy."

Chapter Nine

The facade of Somerset House was imposing, the portal flanked by torches, the wide stairs to the first floor dim. At the top a flunky in white bagwig and black silk formal dress stepped forward and held out a white staff. "No ladies are allowed, ma'am," he intoned severely.

"I am not coming as a lady but as a witness," she told him superbly, but with a sweet smile, and took her father's arm and headed for the open door across the hall.

The boardroom, with walnut paneling supporting large sconces and a glowing chandelier above the long table, was imposing of itself. Most of the armchairs were already filled with formally dressed, elderly gentlemen, with a massive, white-haired man in a larger armchair alone at the head of the table. Lord Ingram guided Chris to him. "Lord Frampton, my daughter Miss Christina Kelway, who has come as a witness," he said firmly.

White eyebrows in a florid face shot up as Lord Frampton rose and bowed.

"Only as a witness and not as a lady," Christina said demurely and curtsied.

"Mighty irregular, Ingram," said the deep voice, "but when the irregularity is so charming, and the situation so unfortunate, I see nothing for it but to acquiesce. Do you sit here at the right side and Miss Kelway beside you. We begin shortly."

"Thank you, my lord, I am expecting two more witnesses," Lord Ingram said matter-of-factly. "May they have chairs?" A snap of the fingers and Chris, turning her head, saw two placed behind her. She looked around the table, at a variety of elderly faces with a variety of expressions as they gazed at her, and then, opposite, at Lord Ashburn and a foxy-faced balding man beside him.

"Thought never had ladies here," barked the balding man.

Lord Frampton nodded, "True, Sisley, but this is a witness."

"So no lady," snickered Lord Sisley.

Lord Frampton bent his head toward him. "Withdraw that and apologize, Sisley." His tone brooked no argument and the fox-faced Sisley muttered something and nodded and Chris removed the restraining hand she had laid on her father's arm. Lord Ashburn had watched the exchange with a bland smile.

Three more gentlemen took chairs and then the factotum beside Lord Ingram intoned, "Your ... guests, sir."

Lord Ingram rose quickly. Turning her back on the table, Chris moved around in her chair, and was proud of her witnesses. Both were in severe evening dress, both looked handsome and distinguished and properly serious until they were greeting her and she was speaking to her father. "You remember the Comte de Oudenard, Father, and with him is Lord Falkner, whom you also know."

Both men bowed. Her father shook hands with the Comte and held out the other to Falkner. "My dear chap. So glad to see you again. Good of you to come. Must see you later."

"Honor. Privilege," intoned the two men as they were introduced to Lord Frampton and took their chairs.

Lord Frampton rapped on the table. "We are met informally, gentlemen, on a peculiar matter that involves the honor and veracity of the two gentlemen on either side of me and of our own honor and standing as a society. As you remember, Lord Ingram has presented to us seventeen rolls of pictures he told me were copies of the pictures, carvings, hieroglyphics of a tomb in Egypt which he had found and where he spent several months on the work. Lord Ashburn had previously presented us with seven rolls of similar pictures that he told us were copied from the temple at Karnak. He now maintains that Lord Ingram's pictures are ill done and inaccurate and so outrageous that he doubts if his lordship was even in Egypt." The strong voice was even, emotionless. "This accusation is unprecedented in our experience. To begin with, we will pass around for each to examine, with all possible speed, the two sets of rolls. Lord Ingram's is the first set."

"Unfair, my lord. Would it not be proper to limit Lord Ingram's—contribution to the same number as furnished by Lord Ashburn?" Lord Sisley demanded.

Lord Frampton paused, then nodded. "Very well. We will pass seven of each gentleman."

Chris sighed. It would take forever to look at the pictures, as a footman laid rolls in front of Lord Sisley, who glanced quickly and snorted and pushed them to the next gentleman. But it all moved very quickly, for no man looked at all the rolls, just one or two of each group, and hurried them along. Her father's came first, and joined the pile on Lord Frampton's left. Then came Lord Ashburn's. Chris looked at one, kept her face stolid, and looked at another, and then unrolled a third and a fourth and the others, then passed them all to her father, without glancing at him or at Lord Ashburn. She heard Lord Falkner stir behind her and lean forward to look over Lord Ingram's shoulder. When the last was laid on the pile Lord Frampton looked at Lord Ashburn.

"Well, sir, what do you wish to say?"

Lord Ashburn shrugged. "It is evident the same types of figures are used in both sets of pictures, for the most part, but the execution is quite different, without the fire and enthusiasm the amazing sights on the walls of great temples cannot but inspire. No one could view these representations of a past glorious civilization without being stirred to the depths, and attempting to convey the emotions aroused. The noble lord's set is dry, done without feeling, as though in a study by lamplight with a few set pieces copied from heaven knows where." He stopped.

Lord Frampton turned his face to Lord Ingram. "Well, sir?"

Chris had been fearful that her father might show some indignation, but Lord Ingram sat relaxed and at ease. "As I understand the charges, my lord, Lord Ashburn states first that he doubts that I was in Egypt and second, even if I were, he doubts that I copied my set of rolls from a real tomb. My daughter beside me shared my months and labors in that distant land."

A murmur of surprise ran around the table.

Christ spoke before anyone could raise an objection. "Yes, my lord, we lived for more than three months in a stone storehouse above the Nile adjacent to the tomb

125

whose walls my father was copying. And I am proud to add that I painted the colors you see on the rolls of my father." She halted lest she say too much.

Lord Sisley waved a heavy hand. "Any daughter would testify as her father wishes. It counts for nothing."

"But," Lord Ingram spoke swiftly before that point of view could be amplified, "two gentlemen have come to speak on my behalf. The Comte de Oudenard called at the storehouse where we lived one evening." He half turned and the Comte rose beside his chair and surveyed the room.

"One evening I was riding along the bank of the Nile, a few miles south of Luxor. I saw a light from a building. It was dark, you understand, the palm trees rustled. I was curious and approached. There I found this gentleman, Lord Ingram, bent over a table that held two lamps, drawing on such a roll of paper as we have seen, drawing with such exquisite care from sketches before him, measuring, reproducing the scenes with a careful delicacy. And beside him Miss Kelway was putting in the colors on a section already completed. The pictures were formidable in their accuracy, for I have seen much of the temples and tombs along the Nile. I was greatly impressed. We exchanged greetings. He showed me what he was doing. I continued my ride. I do not understand how anyone can question the word of Lord Ingram or the authenticity of what he has brought home." He bowed and sat down. Chris wanted to pat his shoulder, but instead merely looked around and smiled gratefully.

"Very vivid," barked a red-faced fat man down the table, "but a Frenchman—in Egypt only a few months ago—special interests, gentlemen, special shall we say plans—wouldn't care to trust them," he ended obscurely.

The Comte started to rise but Lord Frampton shook his head. "There is no need to reply to the insinuations, my dear sir. You told us clearly what you saw. We must leave the judgment to the members of the board. Lord Ingram?"

"The other gentleman," Lord Ingram continued smoothly, "who has been good enough to come here this evening stayed with us at the same stone building. It had four rooms and was doubtless built to hold the gifts, tributes, priests on occasion, needed for the tomb a few yards away where I was copying the wall decorations. Gentlemen, Lord Falkner."

Chris had put the blue taffeta cloak over the back of her chair and knew that it made an effective frame for her and her dress. She had kept her eyes on the table before her but now she raised them and saw Lord Ashburn was regarding Lord Falkner fixedly. When the erstwhile Sidi rose she wondered if she had asked too much of him.

But his voice was smooth, a little deliberate. "I did indeed stay with Lord Ingram and his daughter at the building he has just described to you. Each day we went to the tomb nearby. I was pleased that I was able to secure some planks to put on top of the piles of sand that filled the tomb by nearly a third so that it was easier to stand while copying and making notes than on the shifting sand itself. Lord Ingram copied the figures, the hieroglyphics, measuring the size of each, on a pad he had contrived, and Miss Kelway with her box of paints copied the colors, matching as nearly as possible and noting where each one went. In a few days I was permitted to assist, and I may tell you I was proud when I was allowed to copy some minor figures and even hieroglyphics." Chris could not look up to his face but she saw smiles appear on several of the gentlemen's faces. "I must add, gentlemen, that I am also proud to have been permitted to come to your meeting and to speak of my experience with Lord Ingram." Watching from across the table, Chris was sure Lord Ashburn's face and figure relaxed. She heard a chair shift as Lord Falkner sat down.

"Very conclusive," said one genial voice.

"Not at all," barked Lord Sisley. "Well spoken, yes, can't doubt what he says he saw. But this is all words. We have no proof that Lord Ingram's drawings are exact copies. All those people parading. All those animals in the borders. All those incomprehensible signs. No, sir, I for one am not satisfied."

Lord Frampton swung his head toward Lord Ingram.

For a second he hesitated, then said, "Gentlemen, I could not remove stones from walls—though I understand that has been done by people of other countries—to bring them to show you, nor carry off any of the statues or portions of statues that are lying abandoned in so many spots. But, in my turn, now I have seen Lord Ashburn's own drawings I must cast some doubt on the extent of his knowledge of Egypt and her temples and tombs."

"Trying to smear him, are you?" Lord Sisley said loudly.

Ignoring him, Lord Ingram pointed to the rolls of the Ashburn collection. "You gentlemen have no doubt noticed that on Lord Ashburn's set there appear, in the borders and even once in a chief picture, reproductions of a camel. It is a well-known fact in Egypt that camels do not appear on any temple walls because camels were not introduced into Egypt until the second century before Christ. Also you will have observed that in several pictures the color purple appears on the robes of a chief or priest or lady. The people who built the tombs and temples did not use purple, ever, gentlemen, ever. And furthermore, the faces, limbs of his people are white
128

or faintly pink. The ancient peoples used red for the human skin because they had no color white." He stopped.

"Heard that about camels when I was hunting in Libya," a gruff voice said loudly.

"Painter chap told us once they had no white, used red for faces, thought it odd," contributed a shrill voice.

"Bah," exploded Lord Sisley. "Ingram here is just trying to tar Ashburn with the same mud. There's no real proof. You all know Ashburn is an authority and his pictures are worthy of a place with us and with scholars."

Chris saw two gray heads nod in agreement, her father's hand clench in his lap, and Lord Ashburn smile with satisfaction. She jumped to her feet.

"My Lord Sisley says there is no proof." She began a little loudly to hide the fact her voice was shaking, then brought it down a bit. "There *is* proof, gentlemen." She pulled up the blue knitting bag and plucked out the roll of her own pictures. "These are drawings I made for myself, for my own pleasure, from the walls of a small tomb near the larger one. The chief figure in the wall paintings was a young lady, and she must have loved flowers and animals." She held up one picture, then pushed the roll to the gentleman next to her. "They are obviously not done with the skill of my father, they were just for me. And just the borders, I could not attempt the larger figures."

"Bah," Lord Sisley said loudly again. "You copied his."

She did not deign to look at him. "And here, gentlemen, is proof of the accuracy of my father's figures, which are so much better than mine." She upended the knitting bag and poured a stream of gold on the table. There came gasps, ejaculations of "By Jove," "Gold," "Animals." One by one she set up the figures on the dark polished surface. "These were found by Lord Falkner and myself in the small tomb I mentioned." She waved one hand over them. "You may compare these with any of our drawings if you still have doubts about our accuracy."

Now she stopped and looked around. Lord Ashburn was staring again at Lord Falkner. Her father was smiling proudly and murmuring, "You might have told me," and Lord Falkner was smiling at her in an odd way and the Comte made a silent clap of his hands.

"They must be fake," Lord Ashburn said loudly and forcefully. "Wood with gold leaf on top. You can buy them in the bazaars."

Lord Frampton leaned forward and picked up the cat, looked at Chris inquiringly, and as she nodded removed the single fob from his chain, turned the cat upside down, and scraped at the bottom. The room was silent. He scraped, and scraped again and again.

"Solid gold," he told the waiting faces firmly, restoring the cat to the table and the fob to his chain.

"But," began Lord Sisley.

"Stop." The vigor of the command would have halted a regiment. "I have heard enough, more than enough, of this malicious and infamous attempt to blacken the honor of Lord Ingram. It is evident, and I know I speak for us all," his glance swept up and down the table and there was no dissenting sound, "that Lord Ingram's pictures are accurate and of greatest value and we are honored, I repeat honored, that he has presented them to us for the use of scholars." He halted, bowed to Lord Ingram, who bent his head. "We must apologize that we were led into this buffoonery and caused him and his friends the inconvenience attendant on his coming here this evening at our request. We thank him for the patience and good humor with which he has endured this meeting." There was a flash of a smile as his gaze

130

traveled to Chris. "And we must thank Miss Kelway for coming as a witness and for her very effective production of indisputable proof." He frowned and looked formidable again. "And I beseech you, nay I insist, that no word of what has been said here is to be mentioned to anyone. It is a disgrace to our Society." He flicked a glance at the glowering Lord Sisley. "If I hear even a rumor, and I would hear any such, that this has been mentioned I will take steps, in all of my various capacities, to deal with it and with its perpetrator. Gentlemen, this meeting is adjourned."

Chairs scraped on the floor, voices rose with the gentlemen. Chris stood up and began to replace the little gold figures in the bag. The gentleman next to her handed her her roll and patted her hand. "Well done, Miss Kelway." He beamed at her. "We must all be grateful. Splendid spirit you showed."

Her father was shaking hands with the Comte and Falkner. She turned and held out her hand to Captain or Comte de Oudenard, it did not matter. "You were splendid." Emotion nearly overcame her but she held back the tears that seemed to threaten and smiled. He looked at her, smiled, and nodded, and she nodded back, sealing a bargain, and they shook hands. He spoke to her father, bowed to Lord Frampton, who was thanking him also, and left for the stairs behind the backs of Ashburn and Sisley.

"Glad that's over with," Lord Frampton said expansively. "Nasty business. Apologize again for being led into it. Come have some port with me."

Chris stepped around her father, and held out her hand to Lord Falkner. "Thank you for coming," she said simply. What else was there to say?

He shook her hand as the Comte had. "I am glad I came also. An honor."

Then she heard her father excusing himself from the

port as he must escort his daughter home. Lord Falkner stepped forward. "I will be happy to escort Miss Kelway to Lady Lethbridge's if you permit, sir. I brought my coach with the thought of taking you both."

"Kind of you, sir." Lord Ingram nodded. "Must thank you later, at greater length, for tonight. Yes, of course I'll be glad to have you take Chris back. So," he turned to a genial Lord Frampton, "I may have that port with you after all, sir."

There was nothing Chris could do but go. Falkner scooped the cloak from the chair and placed it around her shoulders and offered his arm. I'm going out in style, she thought, and raised her head even higher, but she would have preferred to make her exit on her father's arm, allies who had won against a nasty enemy. At least the factotum in the white wig bowed low as she passed him.

The coach, dark blue inside and out, was made to seem cozy by two candles enclosed in glass beside the doors. With excited pride now bubbling within her she wished again for her father so they could go over it all and congratulate each other. Now she must show her gratitude again, and then he would have as little inclination to talk as she.

The coach started. She had to speak. "I must thank you once more, my lord, for coming this evening to support my father," she began stiffly.

He looked at her and then away. "You knew I would," he said bluntly. "It was clever to persuade Oudenard also—your doing, I am sure."

"He was most agreeable."

"So you managed us both, and then your own climax." He glanced at the bag in her lap. "It was both theatrical and devastating."

She was not sure that was a compliment, so ignored it. "But why should Lord Ashburn enter into that—

calumny in the first place?" She had forgotten she had no inclination for converse.

He shook his head. "I cannot guess...Unless he feared to lose his place as the present authority on Egypt. Your father obviously knows far more. And the rumor of a possible government appointment for Ashburn has been widespread."

"Perhaps that is his doing," she murmured, and knew he moved his head to glance at her.

There was a moment of silence, but she might as well ask the questions in her mind. "For a moment Lord Ashburn looked startled when I said you and I had found the little figures," she offered. "I wonder why. Perhaps I should have said only you found them, but, but I had to account for my possession."

"Of course. And we did come on them together."

"I should offer you a share now," she suggested, feeling noble just to be saying it.

He cut her off. "Certainly not."

Relieved he had closed that topic so flatly, she had another subject. "Will Lord Ashburn now leave town?" They were conversing in a formal fashion as if they were complete strangers, which she felt, a little forlornly, was only proper.

"Why should he?" He sounded surprised.

"His disgrace—the reprimand—"

"No one will know of that, and no one will reveal it after Lord Frampton's words, for he is a very powerful man. There will be no need for Ashburn to behave in any different fashion from customary."

"Ohhh," she sighed a little. "I suppose he will continue to pursue Audrey."

Even in the strange light of the bobbing candles she could see the eyebrows rise and the wide mouth quirk in almost a smile. "You disapprove? Probably with reason. You will have to turn your managing abilities in that direction, then."

"Stop using that horrid word," she flashed out at him. "I am not managing."

"But my dear Miss Kelway," he mocked. "How can you so hold? You managed your father, Lord Frampton, all those stuffy old gentlemen, Oudenard, Ashburn, and me superbly this evening. I am just giving you all credit for your abilities and success."

"And you do not, from your tone, approve of what I did."

"Oh, I approve of the result, of course, and admired your performance. But," and his tone turned deliberate, "there is nothing more obnoxious than a managing female. My aunt was such a one and I early took the trail in strong dislike."

"I must inform you I do not manage but only act as common sense dictates. But you hold me obnoxious, sir?" she demanded icily.

"That I did not say. If you yourself choose to adopt the word as intended for you—that is your prerogative."

Anger and indigation mounted. "Very well, sir, I do accept it. And where, may I ask, would Sidi have been if I had not managed, there at Clio's tomb, and later?" Bright-eyed she faced him, daring him.

He gave her a long look, and she wished the coach had been bright enough to read his face. "You are right. I forgot, for the moment, your rescue of a starving, dried-out creature who could walk no farther and would soon have made food for the vultures. I am in debt to your management, Miss Kelway."

That was handsomely said but perversely, she would not allow it. "Your forgetting is always convenient, sir. Do you still forget, as you claimed, what it was that brought you to that pass? It must be monstrously comforting to be able to go so in and out of your past."

He did not look away. "I remember the chief, Ibn-El-Hahir," he said evenly, "and my months under him, and what followed. I still do not remember how I came into his power."

"Then you have compounded your forgetting, for you told us you could recall a darkness and firelight on a face and on some gold, and laughing and a blow on your head," she reminded him tartly.

One long hand rubbed across his forehead. "Yes, now you remind me."

"What do you recall came before that?"

"Why," and his voice brightened, "everything, of course, and traveling with Ashburn, enjoying ourselves in Italy, sailing up to Cairo."

"Have you asked Lord Ashburn what happened?"

"Once. He allowed it was a painful subject, but he had saved my life, for I fell prey to one of those strange diseases, went out of my head with fever. He could do nothing for me so he left me with a famous Arab physician in Cairo, they are very good you know, and took half my money to get himself home and gave the rest to the doctor, though I was not supposed to live. That was so different from what I did remember, and so I told him, but he said it was the fever and I had best forget it all. I have not, and I still seek an explanation, perhaps hopelessly. But my life cannot be ordered as I wish, I cannot embark on my plans for the future until I find it."

"You had better fill in that gap before you go around insulting people who helped you." She was still indignant.

"No insult, Miss Kelway. I withdraw that word."

"Weaseling out of it, giving me a Banbury tale to hide your true thoughts. Very well. We are each grateful to the other for certain matters. We dislike each other." She felt the coach pull to a halt. "And we need never discuss anything with each other again."

The coach door opened, steps were let down, he went out the other door and was waiting to give her his arm to mount the stairs to the house.

"I can but bow to your command, and agree with it. But, Miss Kelway, remember I shall always stand ready to be of any possible assistance to your father at any time. Thank you for an instructive evening." He bowed, and as the door opened ran lightly down the shallow steps.

Chapter Ten

Whenever Christina thought of that night drive back with Lord Falkner it was with a vague feeling of dissatisfaction for which she could not account. She had given the noble lord a firm setdown and received his acknowledgment of the debt he owed her. But there were other things to learn—or they should not have had any discussion at all. However, she was made happy by her father's appreciation of her management, though he did not use that hateful word, and he took her out to an elegant dinner and then to a private box at the opera in celebration of the routing of Lord Ashburn. They so enjoyed each other's company they scarcely stopped talking, except during the singing. The only depressing note was that he confirmed that Lord Ashburn would have no need to change his way of life in any way, and would doubtless continue to be regarded as an expert on Egypt.

As proof, Lord Ashburn appeared at Mrs. Dalrimple's breakfast in all his smooth elegance and devoted more than usual of his time to Audrey. He and Miss Kelway exchanged neutral small bows, but he did not come near her then or at the Hodgkinton ball the following week. Audrey seemed more fluttered than before and Chris did not see what she could do to discourage either of them. On the other hand, the Comte de Oudenard, elegant in a yellow satin waistcoat and dark green dress coat, came to Chris for the promenade because, as he explained, it was of greater ease for talking.

"I am happy to be able to thank you again," she began earnestly, but before she could continue he waved one graceful hand as though brushing aside an insect.

"It was a pleasure for which I should thank you, Miss Kelway. Your father is a most admirable gentleman and I find Lord Falkner *très sympathique*. Lord Ashburn is not a nice man, I do not trust him. I was glad to, what do you say, give him a swipe in the eye."

"Yes," she gurgled, "and you did beautifully."

"Even more, Lord Frampton has kindly noticed me and we have enjoyed a dinner together. And, further, it was an opportunity most unusual to see all those august gentlemen, though some do not know as much as they believe." He smiled mischievously. "But I do not so inform them. A foreigner must step carefully as on seashells. I do not always understand your customs. One evening I made a mistake, which I regret and apologize for." He met her startled glance and nodded. "I hope it is forgotten."

"Oh, it has been, I assure you." She wished she could ask him if he had been a comte that night above the Nile, but knew she never could.

"I fear," he sobered a little and sighed, "that I do not advance myself sufficiently in the regards of Miss Cadwell. Lord Ashburn is more overwhelming. But, Miss Kelway, for I count you as a friend, is it not possible to find a wife with a dot sufficiently large in other circles than this?"

"Yes," she said thoughtfully. "It depends on what one seeks, or needs. What have you in mind?" They bowed to a passing couple and she hoped they had not ignored too many.

"I know there are the country, county families, of wealth and standing, who do not visit London, but those it is not likely I will encounter. The other evening I was conducted by a friend to a house on Russell Square. It was a small and pleasant affair. I gather that the Square is the home of many of the important merchants of the city. The young ladies appeared well brought up and some were appealing. But," he asked lightly, "does one marry one of them?"

She nodded, and saw they were so engrossed in their conversation that they could not notice Lord Falkner with Lady Ottilie on his arm. "Indeed, yes. Often enough. A wife from that—that milieu would not be as demanding in some ways perhaps as one who frequents affairs such as this."

"You confirm my own thoughts." It was his turn to nod. "Such a one would not be so *exigeant,* as we say, perhaps a little grateful? Also there would be more of a possibility that I might find something for my energies. I am discovering a life of idleness does not agree with my spirits."

"That I can well believe," she approved. "You might well discover the perfect combination of everything. But I would be careful to learn something of the family—and the business. There I cannot be of help."

"Of course not. You have been of much already. I will ask Sir Alex," he added thoughtfully. "He is always of great kindness to me."

"Do not speak to any but him as you have to me," she warned. "And I wish you luck."

He kissed her hand with a flourish. "Then I will have

it," he declared and they smiled at each other in great amity.

With Lord Falkner she merely exchanged polite bows and told herself that was the most that could be required of either of them. Lady Ottilie was certainly the object of his attentions. Sir Alec confided he was not happy about any possible connection there. "She is not right for Kirby," he said once forcefully, "too worldly, pursues her pleasures." He frowned a moment, then confided he was thinking of something she might enjoy, for a change, and would ask her opinion shortly. As he frequently contrived some new and different entertainment, she allowed she would not draw breath until she knew, which he advised against, and chuckled as he left her.

There was a slight flurry one day at the Lethbridge house. A messenger girl, bringing three hats from Madame Seraphine, had offered to carry them to the ladies' rooms and then been discovered by Rose, who thought she was taking too long a time, rummaging through the drawers of Chris's dressing table. She was bustled away, taken back in a hackney by Mrs. Pritchett to Seraphine, and promptly fired. It was no loss, Madame herself explained, for she had only been hired that morning. The girl had turned sullen and given no explanation but curiosity. Madame apologized profusely, complained of the impossibility of finding the right kind of girls to do errands, and it was all forgotten.

Perhaps the dramatic account from the Salon des Chapeaux had lingered with Chris, for suddenly, while dancing with Sir Alec at the Ammonton ball, she asked, "Is not the amount of crime much greater in the city than in the country?"

He no longer schooled his face in her company so his surprise showed. "It is a question, I confess, to which I have not given any thought. Without doubt there is more in volume, so to speak, in the city because of the greater population, but I presume there is just about the same, in proportion, in the countryside."

Country. Chris turned her head and faced into the room and sniffed the familiar combination of dust, melting wax, perfumes, a touch of kerosene from lamps at the entrance. In the country it would be so fresh. "May we go walk on the balcony for a moment? Fresh air would be welcome."

In four steps he had her out the nearest French window and on the long balcony. From the blackness before them came the damp fresh scent of wet earth. It was misting and no evening to suggest strolls among bushes. "In the country now, it would be all green," she sighed. "And it would smell better."

He laughed and led her back to the room.

She and Sir Alec had returned to Lady Lethbridge when a young man in full evening rig but with color in his face that showed he spent his time out in all weather approached. "May I introduce myself, my lady? I am James Purvis of Stadings in Sussex. Lady Frances Outram recommended that I bring myself to your attention."

Lady Lethbridge held out her hand, which was bowed over with a grace that belied the stalwart figure. "And I am glad you have, Mr. Purvis, for she wrote me you would be in London, and suggested I ask you to call, which I am happy to do."

"I thank you, ma'am," he said as he straightened. "I . . ."

A little shriek of delight interrupted him. "Jim," Audrey cried, and rushed to his side. "Jim, I am glad to see you. Did you come to see me?"

He took the outstretched hand and, smiling a little, kissed it briefly. "Why, not particularly, I must confess,

Miss Cadwell. I am come to town on business for my father, but seeing you is a reward."

Audrey pouted. "You should have come before this, and to see me, and how well I go on here in London. And stop being fustian. You have called me Audrey for all these years and I do not see why you should turn formal."

"You are become such a grand lady now I could not venture to remind you of our—friendship, without your permission." He spoke solemnly but there was a gleam in the brown eyes. "To affirm that friendship, then, Audrey, may I have the pleasure of taking you to supper?"

For a moment Audrey looked confused and withdrew the hand both had forgotten. "Oh, I am so sorry, that is already bespoken, but . . ."

"Then may I look forward to a dance later?" He was so cheerful that Audrey could not hide her surprise. He murmured "your servant" to Lady Lethbridge and moved away.

"What an attractive young man," exclaimed Lady Lethbridge.

Audrey tossed her head. "He is only Jim Purvis, a neighbor, who prefers the country to the city. I did not know," and she frowned a moment, "he had such social graces for the city."

"You know now," Lady Lethbridge said with asperity. "Sir Alec, I recommend him to you, for dear Lady Outram wrote of him with great enthusiasm."

As Mr. Bowman claimed his dance, Chris heard the two still speaking of Squire Purvis' son, and laughed.

Two days later, Sir Alec called to beg her and Audrey to join a small party he was forming for just three nights at his home, Bouton Abbas in Hampshire. It would be small, only fourteen, and informal, he explained, for it was quite in the country. The only entertainment he could offer, aside from what they evolved themselves, was a ducal dance on Saturday night, but the air would be salubrious and the brief change from London would, he hoped, be welcome. Since Mr. Purvis was on hand, he was included in the invitation. Sir Alec's aunt, Mrs. Southwick, who lived in the place, would be chaperone, he assured Lady Lethbridge. Chris and Mr. Purvis accepted instantly, Audrey a little more slowly.

On returning from the ball where Mr. Purvis entered society she had expressed herself vigorously to Chris on his lack of conduct in saying openly he had not come to the city on purpose to see her, on his not having come sooner, on his having objected to the infrequency of her letters and to her subject matter, and at his being not at all disturbed that he could not take her to supper and she hoped he had seen her with Lord Ashburn but had not been sure, and that surely he would come tomorrow to call. She had been annoyed again when he had not. And, when he did, he remained as agreeably formal with her as with the other ladies he had not known all these years.

Lady Lethbridge loaned her own coach to the girls, and with Rose almost speechless with excitement on the box seat, they arrived well before tea. Bouton Abbas, of gray stone and long windows, obviously made from the ruins that could be discerned at a little distance, contrived to be both impressive and delightful. Lawns and gardens spread on all sides, backed by high elms, and, since the Abbas was on a rise, a view to the south, as was always desired. Chris admired it unreservedly as Sir Alec escorted her from the coach to the wide door, and touched her hand as it lay on his arm.

"I am happy it pleases you, Miss Kelway. And would you be good enough to join me there in the rose garden, to the left, in ten minutes or so? I would like to explain something . . ." His voice trailed away. At her inquiring look he shook his head.

Cloak and bonnet discarded, and Rose directed to the unpacking, Chris discovered, aided by a footman, the French side windows that led to the walled rose garden. She crossed a terrace, went down some steps, and stopped. Evidently it had rained recently, for an occasional drop still hung, glinting from leaf and spray. The scent of turned dark earth, fresh-cut grass, of woods brought by a breeze, all carried her back to her childhood days when such had been a welcome part of her life, and so common as to be unnoticed. She could not hurry down the white marble-chip path to the waiting figure by an arbor, and she could not prevent the tears from rising.

Sir Alec strode forward quickly and seized her hands. "My dear. What is wrong? You are unhappy . . . ?"

She let her hands rest in his and smiled apologetically. "No. Forgive me. It is just as it should be in the country. It smells so *right*. I've been away from it for so long. I am quite myself, I promise you." She let him guide her to the arbor, where two cushions had been placed on seats that must be wet. "I'm glad to be here," she ended by way of atonement.

"And I to have you." He paused and for the first time she saw embarrassment on his fine-featured face. "I had hoped to enjoy these days with you. But I am, so to speak, hoist with my own petard. I had planned that you would be my chief guest. But in a mistaken moment I invited Lady Sarah Bagley because I had spent a pleasant week at her father's place in Gloucestershire. I never thought she would come. To my distress, she accepted, and, as you recognize, since she is of the highest rank among the guests, it is she I must escort and place at my right hand and do the honors." He looked abashed and regretful and embarrassed, and she burst out laughing.

"Oh, dear Sir Alec, do not look so. Of course I understand. I am flattered that you thought of me that way, but naturally Lady Sarah, a duke's daughter, has first claim to your attentions. I shall contrive famously, I am sure."

To her surprise a look of slight affront replaced his embarrassment. "I so hope," he said stiffly, then gave her a tentative look. "I must confess I asked another guest here in the hope I could contrive if not a reconciliation, too strong a word no doubt, an amelioration of what has seemed to me a certain coldness between you and Kirby Derwent, Lord Falkner that is. You are both my good friends and I am distressed that you might have fallen out of charity with each other. I hope that here, removed from London, you might discover how much you have in common and become friends."

A facer, Chris thought, and contrived a smile as she looked over the neat green bushes. "You are kind to notice," she began carefully, "but it is not a serious matter. It is simply that we found we did not have so much to say to each other as we had thought. And Lord Falkner is popular. He has no need of my company."

His dubious look showed he was not satisfied but too polite to protest. "Since it is nothing but missing opportunities, why, I hope you both will find subjects of mutual interest."

It was better to leave on that note, she decided, and rose, and admired the garden and this view of the house, and left to change for tea before he had a chance to inquire further, hoping he would have the good sense not to force her and the distant Lord Falkner together.

Audrey was overflowing with conversation as she surveyed her wardrobe for the proper dress. She had been for a walk, or just to the edge of the woods, with

145

a Mr. Andrew Walden, who was delightful. Sir Alec had certainly assembled a charming group of guests, she had never been to a house party before and had not realized how delightful it could be. How selfish Lord Ashburn had been when he pressed her not to come because he was not invited. She had told him with some heat she could not insult dear Sir Alec in that fashion. Ashburn had almost showed some temper and would be even more annoyed when he learned that Jim Purvis was of the party. She giggled and almost decided on a simple dark green dress as appropriate for the country.

Chris hastily substituted a dark blue for the green she had chosen and escaped. Audrey was a dear, but she was inclined to be scatterbrained at times. Bouton Abbas was too large a house to explore on one's own, but she might find the library, which should be interesting, and a place that might be useful for a retreat. As she wandered across the high entrance hall, tastefully hung with rather dim tapestries, she heard some vehicles arriving and hastened down an adjacent corridor. She had no desire to meet anyone until she had to. First she stumbled on two saloons, pale green and pale yellow, and by leaving them by the far door did find the library. It was sunlit, comfortable, and as she had expected, walled with books.

She was moving along one wall, touching with one finger a book she recognized, or would care to read someday, when a pleasant voice said, "Miss Kelway, will you grant me a few minutes?"

"Mr. Purvis, of course. I was only contemplating some old friends and would vastly prefer new ones," she bantered, and went toward a wide bay window with a red cushioned seat that looked out on the garden she had recently left.

Mr. Purvis sat down beside her, then moved backward so he could draw up one leg and clasp his arms around it, an informal posture she was sure foretold confidences. "I would not consult with you on my own, ma'am, but Lady Lethbridge advised me to speak openly with you about my problem."

"Then it is about Audrey," she offered.

"Of course. In spite of what I told her, you heard, I did come to London to see her and what she is up to." His grin was a little guilty. "I was sure it would not do to tell her so. I had already thought of my tactics, and her aunt improved on them. Audrey is a dear girl." He leaned forward a little and spoke earnestly. "But she can be, well, flighty at times. I have long loved her, wished to marry her, for I know I can keep her safe and make her happy. But it is evident this London visit has not improved my chances."

Chris looked at him with some compassion. He was obviously a thoroughly nice man, and just what Audrey needed. "She has been the object of considerable attention, sir," she began.

"Oh, I know that. And her head has been turned." He was quite serious about it. "But often I have seen her change her mind and come to desire something which it seems she cannot have."

"Yourself, sir?"

He looked embarrassed. "I do not set myself up as any prize in the marriage mart, believe me, Miss Kelway. I am well aware of all the objections of Audrey's mother, which are valid, from her point of view. But I do know I am right for Audrey and that no one could love or cherish her more, or be less demanding, or make her happier."

Chris felt herself glowing at him. No man could speak with that fervor and not feel deeply. "Oh, my dear sir, I know you are right. I am flattered you have told me."

"Then would you help me? It is this," and he rushed

on, not waiting for her answer. "May I pay you attentions these next days? No one could wonder, you are so charming. And you would not object that they are not serious? I felt it only proper to explain my position to you. Not that I think you would ever consider my attentions serious, for I know I am not in your field, but I knew I must ask so that it could be quite comfortable between us." He turned anxious. "You do not have any gentleman in whom you have, well, a special interest of your own whom I might, well, obstruct?"

"No, there is no one," she began, and without a shade of regret, and then gave a spurt of laughter. "Of course I will not object. I shall be flattered by your attentions. Shall I show a slight, very slight, inclination in your direction?" He grinned again, but a little uncertainly. "Do not mind my laughter. I think it is an excellent notion, and I believe it will work, though Audrey is a pea-goose to make it necessary. For her own sake we will conspire . . . and to make it a bit more evident suppose we come to first-name terms immediately?"

His brown eyes were twinkling now. "That I appreciate, and I cannot tell you how happy I am that you agree. There is no fellow conspirator I could enjoy more."

If that sounded a little pompous she could forgive him, for he was evidently happy and more at ease. "Why, thank you, sir. Let us go and commence by finding the tea party, Jim," and she gurgled again, as he jumped to his feet and held out his arm.

Tea, presided over by plump, comfortable, amused Mrs. Southwick, was more lively than customary, for all persisted in standing and moving around to talk with each guest. Lady Sarah proved to be a tall, handsome girl, with straight hair that escaped in wisps from the braids around her head, and such an open cheerful countenance Chris was drawn to her instantly. Undoubtedly Lady Sarah could drive her pair to an inch and sustain the rigors of a day fox hunting, but her voice was low and pleasing and she was genuinely friendly and at home with all. Jim was attentive beyond his duty and once when they were laughing together Chris, in a mirror, saw Audrey watching them and felt it a good beginning. She noticed that Lady Sarah appropriated Lord Falkner, but in a nice way.

Chapter Eleven

At dinner Lady Sarah was on Sir Alec's right, with Lord Falkner next to her and then Chris with Jim on her right. Now Audrey's suitor had lost any embarrassment he was increasingly easy to talk with and she found herself liking him more and more. When the time came to turn to Lord Falkner on her left she felt Sir Alec's eyes rest on her for a second, so she smiled agreeably and asked about the trip from London, a safe topic. They could both enlarge on that, and did, for the requisite minutes, and then, duty done, smiled and turned away. The evening was spent playing whist, or less exacting card games for the uninitiated. Jim Purvis partnered Chris whenever possible, and when free, took a chair behind her to direct her play.

When the games broke up for the tea table and she took a place on a sofa, to her surprise it was Lord Falkner who brought her cup and took the place beside her, just ahead of an approaching Jim, who veered sharply away and sought Audrey.

Lord Falkner looked faintly amused. "He's a sound man," he said, "and since you have accorded him the privilege of using your first name, and on such short acquaintance, could I not be allowed the same pleasure? After all, our ... acquaintance goes back several months." He bent his head with an inquiring look.

For a moment Chris was taken aback. Jim, after all, had a purpose and Falkner none but to be annoying. She rallied quickly. "Why, certainly, my lord. So I may call you Kirby? It will be vastly easier than Lord Falkner, I confess, and may banish Sidi, which occasionally comes to my tongue."

"I am not surprised," he said softly, eyes hooded. "And Chris seems quite natural to me, for I once heard it so often."

She knew they were both remembering sand and moonlight and palm trees and the Nile, which brought back other things also. "I am aware of your condescension," she said stiffly, to avoid memory.

"Oh, stop being like that," his voice lazily good-humored. "You're not at all. You'd prefer to give me a setdown, but I won't let you. What was Purvis entertaining you with at dinner?"

"His days at Oxford," she answered without hesitation. "He enjoyed himself there."

"Most of us do. Remind me to recount some of my own. I trust all is well with your father?"

"Indeed; he is enjoying himself more than ever." At that moment Mrs. Southwick rose, and the guests with her, the ladies to seek their rooms, leaving the gentlemen to their own brand of entertainment. It was Jim Purvis who handed her her candle with a whisper. "We are doing famously, dear Christina."

At the picnic lunch the next day there was no possibility for pairing, if that was desired. It was held at the ruins of the monastery from which Bouton Abbas had been built, and as it was surrounded by fields of growing hay there was no temptation to stroll beyond the cut turf within the low straggling walls. The stones in the cloister, where the hampers were brought by footmen, were quite too hard, even when topped by cushions, for anyone to enjoy sitting for long, which Chris was sure Sir Alec knew full well. So all strolled around, drumstick in one hand, sandwich in another, to exclaim at the empty Gothic tracery of the few remaining windows and the view over meadows to woods and hills. Lady Sarah and Chris climbed together the winding stair of the tower, whose top two floors were missing, and leaning on the parapet giggled together at the unusual sight of a party seen from above. It was all languorous and pleasing and the fresh air put the guests into the proper frame of a nap before tea and dressing.

The ducal estate, ten miles away, was of imposingly chill Palladian style but was graced with a handsome ballroom in one wing. For this Chris had donned her best blue ball gown with sequins edging the spangled overskirt and sleeves and square neck. At the last moment she daringly fastened a two-inch strand of the sequins, brought in case of need, into the curls above her left ear, and smiled at the effect. Audrey looked her best in a rather billowing pink and Lady Sarah was particularly handsome in an amber silk.

It was a large ball, with obviously, the gentry of the county in attendance. Jim claimed her for the first dance and Sir Alec for the second, having done his duty by Lady Sarah. They appeared easy friends, but nothing more, Chris thought. For the third dance Lord Falkner, in a claret-colored jacket that had been admired by the other men, came to claim her. She was relieved it was one of those country dances where sustained conversation is impossible. She did think that it was a little lowering that of the two men who were paying her attention one had ulterior purposes and the other was under some sort of compulsion, for she was convinced Sir Alec had spoken to Falkner as he had to her.

She was standing by a window jesting with Audrey when she became conscious of movement in the room to her right and half turning was confronted by an imposing figure of green and blue and red in kilt and plaid. "Miss Kelway," Sir Alec was saying beside her, "may I present Sir Angus MacLennan, who has expressed a desire to meet you?"

There was nothing to do but curtsy to the impressive bow, and allow herself to be led into the nearest figure forming on the dance floor. "I saw you from the doorway," said a deep voice above her, "and I knew you were the one lady I wished to meet."

She looked up into bright gray eyes. "Why?"

"Because you have the look of a girl who'll get up and do anything, go anywhere that appeals to you, a lively look, I might say. I have not seen it often in your country, but then," he added fairly, "I have only been a few days south of the border."

"How did you know?" His directness was breathtaking.

"It's a look I see at times in the ladies of my own land, though more in those from the north than the south. There's a glint in your eyes that matches the glint in your hair. And besides, you are more interesting-looking than pretty, as was that blond girl beside you."

"Why, I'm flattered, sir," she managed, and then laughed with pleasure. Here was a man who had chosen her for herself.

He laughed with her. "No need to be, ma'am. I speak but the truth. Do you know my country?"

When she confessed ignorance he began to enlighten her, when they met in the dance, but obviously found that not satisfactory. "We will stroll outside for the next dance," he informed her as that one ended. "One cannot converse when moving rapidly in every direction." He began to steer her toward an open window and the terrace beyond.

"I say, pardon me." It was Mr. Walden blocking their way. "I was promised a dance. You can't have two dances in succession with the same girl, you know."

Sir Angus MacLennan looked down at him superbly. "I do not so know. That is some ridiculous Sassenach ruling," the r's rolling impressively. "It does not apply to the MacLennan." One arm did not quite brush Mr. Walden aside but the other firmly took Chris through the window to the terrace. Once there he stopped. "That was perhaps not the right thing to do?" he asked anxiously. "But I did not mean to lose you so quickly."

"It is unusual but delightful, dear sir," Chris gurgled. "But let us move away from that window lest he follow."

"He'll not dare," but he marched several steps, still holding her arm. They fell to a slow pace and Sir Angus proved a quiet and charming companion. He was visiting nearby, he told her, and on his way to Kent—to London he refused to go—and then to France to search for some relatives. "I belong to a sect of the Camerons," he told her with pride, as though that explained everything, and Chris made a note to ask her father what all that was about. He amused her with his opinions of the England he had seen so far. It was the first time he had been in a foreign land, he explained, and spoke with a homesick note of the beauties of the Highlands.

"Why, I feel like Desdemona," she exclaimed as he paused for a moment.

"Nay, I'm no Othello, ma'am, in any way, except perhaps for a liking for a good fight. That's one of the things we Scots do best," he added matter-of-factly.

Not knowing whether to praise or chide, Chris was

relieved of deciding when quick steps approached. "Christina!" It was Lord Falkner. "I've been looking for you and was told there was a successful raid across the border. But you've been here for two dances. It won't do, you know."

Sir Angus bent a little. "Is that true?" he whispered.

"I'm sorry to say it is, sir," she whispered.

He straightened. "Then the raid is being halted, for the nonce, sir. We will return to the ball," and he offered Chris his arm. She felt her entrance, even if through a window, flanked by Sir Angus and Lord Falkner, was nothing less than a royal progress, and agreed, a little aloofly, to dance with his lordship.

He looked at her oddly. "Why, you're glowing," he murmured. "I never saw you in such vivid looks."

"But you have not seen me often, sir," she pointed out with some reason, and was pleased to know she did indeed look well.

Never, she told herself a little later, would she have such an enjoyable evening, for the three men definitely pursued her. Sir Angus was a darling, but definitely not for her, though she had no idea how many of the extravagant compliments he paid were meant. Then, when Sir Alec put Falkner aside and claimed a dance she had an inspiration. Lady Sarah and Falkner were dancing amiably together. Sir Alec twitted her about her conquest of the wild Scot, and vowed he would be jealous if the man stayed another day in the neighborhood.

"No, no, Sir Alec," she said thoughtfully. "There would be no need. But has it not occurred to you that Sir Angus and Lady Sarah might deal exceptionally well together?"

He held her away from him, his gaze admiring. "By Jove, my dear, you are right. I'll see to it. After all, the poor fellow needs some variety this night, now."

"Of course," she agreed sweetly. "I was sure you would see the need."

It was his turn to laugh and call her a minx. But the next dance she saw Sir Angus and Lady Sarah talking with vivacity, and making the most handsome couple in the room.

Audrey was very silent as they undressed, and Chris could not but be glad there was no inclination to discuss the evening.

The glow of the ball lingered with her the next morning and brought a restlessness. She would enjoy a walk, she decided, and another chance to sniff the country air and perhaps scuff up last year's leaves for the dank sweetness that brought. She came down for breakfast, and enjoyed a good one, that included, to her amusement, Scotch kippers, and went to put on walking shoes. When she came down again there was no one in sight but Mrs. Southwick, still presiding at the breakfast table for two latecomers. She waved from the doorway and said she was going for a short walk, and went out the front door and around to the right, away from the rose garden to a path that led to some woods. The woods were well kept but a sufficiency of dead leaves remained for scuffing, and she wandered on, enjoying bird sounds, one a lark, and the peace around her. The character of the woods changed abruptly, but the path was clear and she followed it idly, telling herself she should go back at the next curve.

At the next curve, around some bushes, a man confronted her, bearded, shaggy, in ragged dirty clothes, carrying over his shoulder a bag, from which protruded an ear of what was undoubtedly a rabbit, and a gun in his hand.

"What are you doing here, miss?" he asked in a rough country voice. "Not spying on poor Hal."

156

"I don't know what you mean," she returned coldly. "I'm just on a walk."

"And all alone in the woods, now. 'Tis strange for a young lady to do such, unless she hopes to meet someone."

A faint prickle ran up her spine. "Of course others are joining me." She kept her voice casual, and looked around her on either side of the path.

The man took a step nearer. "There's no sound of 'em. And you've met ol' Hal, and he's man enough for any lass."

"You're poaching," she said severely, "and it's not the season for rabbits."

"Seasons don't matter to Hal, but pretty girls do." His small eyes narrowed. "No, you're alone, me dear, which is just right."

"Don't come near me," she ordered. "I won't tell I saw you."

"Wouldn't matter if you did, no one touches ol' Hal." He took another step. She knew in these long skirts she could not hope to outrun him. She had seen a tree she could use. He came closer still, his back to the thick clump of bushes. One more step he made and was almost right at her. She put up her hands, jumped forward, and shoved hard. He was caught off guard and unbalanced by sack and gun. He sat down in the tangle of branches, the gun falling from his hand. She whirled and ran to the tree, which was made for climbing. She could reach the bottom branch. She swung herself up, raised her arms, and pulled herself to the next branch, and by a step on another, hiking up her skirts to make that, she reached yet another, where she sat down beside the trunk. The man below was on his feet, glaring up at her.

"Think to fox ol' Hal? I'm a-comin' up after you."

"Don't be so foolish," she called down. "The branches won't bear your weight and you'll fall and break a leg."

That gave him pause. He looked at her, at the path, at the gun, and eased himself down again in front of the bushes. "Then I'll wait for you to come down. 'Tis more comfortable a-settin' here than on that stick you're on." She had never knowingly seen a leer but she was sure that was what he gave her.

"You'll have a long wait," she called back, and settled herself a little more comfortably, and heard footsteps.

"Come. Help," she called as loudly as she could and had the satisfaction of hearing the footsteps begin to run and seeing ol' Hal begin to look uneasy. As she turned to look, the steps halted and Lord Falkner came into view.

"Miss Kelway, Christina, what are you doing in a tree?"

"It's safer than on the ground, as you can see," she snapped. "Pray dispose of that object."

"Certainly." He stood in the middle of the path, his head turning from the tree to ol' Hal, who was struggling to rise. The gun lay on the ground between them. "What's the matter?"

A mumble came from the beard. "Ain't nothin'."

"I was walking along and that—that thing came around the bushes and said I was spying on him and then that I'd come to meet someone and ol' Hal was man enough for any lass and he came up to me so I jumped and pushed him down hard and ran and climbed the tree. Now he says he's waiting for me to come down."

Falkner bent his gaze on the rising figure and, obviously, on the sack. "Poaching?" he asked pleasantly.

"This is Hopping Wood, don't no one own it. Frayfield land stops back there. You can't do nothin'," he began to bluster.

"Do make him go away," she begged.

"You better leave, my man." Falkner was still pleasant as he took two long steps and placed one foot squarely on the gun.

"Didn't mean no harm." Ol' Hal began to whine. "Just goin' to have a bit of fun. No law agin it, in woods."

"You'll find there is. Now, get out, fast." The voice whipped across the space.

Ol' Hal gave him a startled glance, looked at the gun on the ground. "You wouldn't keep me gun, mister. All I got to keep from starvin'."

"You'll find it at the end of the path. Now get."

Though Falkner was standing easily there must have been something in the face Chris could not see that warned the man, for the awkward figure, clutching the sack, turned and shambled quickly away.

Falkner picked up the gun and swung around to face her. "That looks quite comfortable," he remarked. "It is years since I climbed a tree." He set the gun against the trunk, jumped, and swung himself up on a branch on the opposite side, rose, stretched, and moved up again until he was resting on a branch a little below her. "I am relieved to find I still can. You, I see, had no doubts. And you managed with your usual aplomb."

The branch he was sitting on grew out at an angle to hers so they nearly faced each other. He was laughing, openly, which she could not but resent. And suddenly he was looking like Sidi of the days on the Nile, or at least his expression did, though he was also unmistakably Lord Falkner, and she was not sure which she was watching. Then she was responding to his laughter with a spurt of her own. "I wasn't managing.

It was just common sense, to seek the nearest refuge. It was all horrid."

"Oh, undoubtedly. A lesson to you, my girl, not to go walking in strange country alone. Mrs. Southwick sent me after you for you had set out with such a determined stride she feared you would stray far from Frayfield land."

"I am grateful to her, and to you." She laughed again. "What a sight I must have presented, perched in a tree, when you came down the path." She put up one hand to straighten her hair, felt herself teeter a little, and replaced it quickly on the branch beside her.

"Unusual, one might say," and his eyes were sparkling with amusement. "Now whenever I go in a wood I will find myself inspecting each tree, hoping another pretty girl will be ensconced."

"Unwise, think of all the birds you will miss." She teetered again. The branch beneath her was narrow and very hard. It would be too ignominious to fall. "Now I would like to get down," she said firmly.

"Why? The view is, well, interesting. We may never be in a tree together again. We should make the most of it." He was laughing even more openly.

"You are being unsympathetic, and perverse," she told him uneasily. The branch beneath her was growing harder and narrower every minute.

"No, no," he soothed. "I am just enjoying the sensation of being a knight-errant and rescuing a beautiful maiden. And," his gaze traveled down from her face, "enjoying the view."

She followed his gaze and saw with horror that, having pulled up her dress so she could climb from branch to branch and then settle by the trunk, she had neglected to pull down her skirts. Her legs, cased in pale silk stockings, were dangling from the knees. She couldn't have pulled down the dress, she told herself
160

angrily. She tried to shift from side to side to lower the garment, but she was sitting on it too firmly and too free movement might be disastrous to her balance.

"Don't wiggle so," he advised. "Your legs are as pretty as I had presumed."

She knew she blushed for his laughter deepened. "You should not mention legs," she admonished loftily.

"How can I avoid it, when you display them before me, and to such advantage?" he reproached.

"You are impossible. I wish to get down."

"Very well. Shall I stand beneath you and catch you as you drop? Anything to oblige."

"No." That would be too undignified. "You may descend yourself and stand with your back to me while I climb down."

"There is no need to be in such a hurry." He looked again at her legs and laughed once more. "But, very well, your servant, ma'am." He turned, swung himself down, and stood with his back to the tree. She turned cautiously, felt with one foot for the next branch, and felt her dress descend around her, moved down one, reached a foot for the next and missed, and tumbled into arms swiftly uplifted to catch her. She lay there for a moment, looking up into face and eyes alight with laughter. "Just what I hoped for," he said and the face came down and he was kissing her mouth very firmly. It was the first time a man had kissed her and she found it unexpectedly pleasant. He lifted his head. "The knight's reward," he murmured, and suddenly set her on her feet. "You have suffered no harm?" he demanded, laughter gone.

For a moment she clung to his arm with both hands to steady herself, and knew she must treat it all with lightness. "Only to my dignity," she gasped, and dropped his arm.

"Then not at all." After a watchful moment he went

and picked up the gun, then took her arm to the path. It was narrow, and he went ahead without a word. She knew she was disheveled but there was nothing she could do about it. She walked slowly and was grateful that he suited his pace to hers. At the edge of Hopping Wood he stopped and thrust the gun, barrel down, deep into the earth.

"He'll come and find it," she said vengefully, "too quickly."

"Yes, but it will take him so long to clean the barrel he'll not use it this day." He looked at her with a critical air. "Dishevelment becomes you, I must say; such pretty hair," he added solemnly. "And you will now remember that when I regard you, even in the most elegant of gowns, I will be seeing your legs beneath them, and enjoying the memory."

"Oh," she gasped, hands flying to her cheeks. "You are abominable. I—I too will remember," and a wail came into her voice.

"No one could appreciate them more, I assure you. I..."

She whirled and began to walk as fast as she could through the Frayfield woods. He came up with her, caught her hand, and tucked it inside his arm. "Perhaps we will both forget," he offered. "And I did send ol' Hal away. You might have been in that tree till sundown."

That was very true. She stopped again. "Yes, and I deeply thank you again, sir, for bringing so neatly to an end an unpleasant situation."

"You are welcome. It was a pleasure. No, no, don't bridle. A man is always happy to display his abilities before an admiring female. And I wish to say that I think you managed with admirable clearheadedness and fortitude, for that man could have become a very nasty customer."

She was gratified by his expressing her own opinions. She could not help glowing at him and saying "Yes," with enthusiasm.

"And we'll ignore it all and say nothing of the—adventure," he continued. Agreeing, Chris felt quite sure that Sidi and Lord Falkner had now rolled into one person.

Tea, from a staid beginning, turned into a surprisingly bustling and crowded affair, with strangers arriving with varied excuses and departing quickly or settling down for a discussion with friends and no knowing who they were or why they had really come except that it was all with a holiday, exuberant air that could not but be diverting. Chris was standing by a window rallying with Jim and some unknown but agreeable man when a deep voice said above her, "Miss Kelway. I knew I was right to come, to see you by daylight."

Still laughing she looked up. "Sir Angus. How agreeable to see you again." And it was, even though he and Lady Sarah had so obviously dealt well with each other. "You should have had no doubts, you know, or believe one changes between night and day. You do remember Mr. Purvis." She gestured to him. "And . . . " The other man muttered a name, bowed, and edged away.

"Aye. I remember Mr. Purvis verrrry well," and Sir Angus bent a stern look at her companion.

"And I you, sir," Jim responded cordially, "and so, forgive me . . . " and with an amused look at Chris he left them.

"It is agreeable to find a man who can take a hint without rancor," observed Sir Angus seriously. "You are not involved with him?"

She managed to choke out, "Oh, no, sir."

"Nor with any other gentleman?" His head was bent as he watched her face.

This time she was prepared and waved an airy hand

for him to read as he may. "Indeed, sir, the questions are out of the ordinary."

"So am I," he agreed, "and if I seek knowledge I must ask directly, for there is no time." He shifted his gaze to look around the room. "A most agreeable house," he commented, "as is its owner. A good friend for you, but no more? Miss Kelway, I made Apthorp bring me here on our way to two other engagements which I would avoid but canna. We are friends and he visits often," he added as if that explained everything, as indeed it did. "But one canna talk in the midst of sounds as of three hunting packs. You leave tomorrow? I do also. Would you come riding with me at seven of the morning, for an hour? You have your riding garb?"

"Why, yes." Lady Lethbridge had told her always to take it on a weekend even if riding was not specified, for one never knew when it might come to have some use. A ride in the morning with this nice man would be very enjoyable. "I'd be happy to join you," she said sedately, but looking very pleased at the notion. "I am sure Sir Alec could mount me."

"No need to trouble him or his stables. I found a mare at Apthorp's which will suit you and I'll bring her with me. At seven, then, in the front, for I know no other approach."

"That approach will be most convenient, sir, and I look forward to the ride." She was surprised at the intent look in his eyes.

"You make all I must go through this evening worthwhile," he began with utmost seriousness, "and I trust..."

"MacLennan, good to see you again," said the easy voice of Lord Falkner. "I trust your stay in England will permit a few days in London. Permit me to put you up, sir, if that should come about."

"You are most kind to a stranger, sir," Sir Angus

answered a little guardedly, "but my stay in England is as short as possible."

"Pity. May I bring you a drink now, then? Or a cup of tea, Miss Kelway?" Either, or both, he intimated, would bring him pleasure.

Sir Angus watched him seriously. "You are acquainted with Miss Kelway, I take it?"

Falkner laughed. "Oh, indeed, for some months, but..."

"Angus, tear yourself away like a good chap." A bright-faced sandy-haired man had a hand on the Scot's arm. "Hard, I know, but we're committed..."

"Then, of course." Sir Angus bowed solemnly to Chris, and to Falkner, and followed his host.

"Good chap," remarked Lord Falkner, watching the pair thread their way through the crowded room. "Apthorp says a splendid sportsman."

"I am sure he is." Chris gave a spurt of laughter, and they were separated by two unknown guests making the rounds. But how nice to be so sought out, she thought, as she listened to praise of Hampshire. The tryst, for she did think of it that way, for tomorrow brought her added amusement at the attentions of Jim Purvis and Lord Falkner, and again she was gratified that someone had sought her out instead of being constrained to do so as were these two.

There were light showers during the night, just enough to leave the lawns a sheet of sparkles and to lay the dust of the roads. Theta, the chestnut filly, was a dainty friendly charmer and Sir Angus such a magnificent figure on a black that Chris regretted they were not heading for the afternoon promenade, where he would create a stir. She had been waiting for him at the steps in front, and he had lifted her into the saddle with only a good morning but an appreciative glow in his eyes that told her she was looking as well in her blue habit as she hoped. At the gates they turned right into a blossom- and bird-filled morning and it was so enchanting Chris threw back her head and laughed and exclaimed and moved Theta into a trot and then a long easy canter, with Sir Angus holding his mount level with hers and guiding her from road to lanes and then, in spite of her reproachful glance, slowing down to a walk.

"A beautiful morning indeed, Miss Kelway," he began, turning to talk with her, "and no man could be more fortunate in his companion, who so matches and enjoys it."

"Why, thank you, sir." She could not look demure and found herself laughing again. "I thank you, for the morning of course."

"I begged for it," he began a little heavily, "because I had so much I wished to say to you and so little time, even now."

"How regrettable that you have to leave, Sir Angus," she said impulsively, "though no delight in London could match this ride."

"It is that which I must explain," he went on slowly. "I must to France. I have many commissions, errands to perform, letters to deliver, some, you must understand, involving those who fled after the disaster of '45 and their descendants. There is need for hurry in some cases. I am honor-bound. You understand?" He leaned forward and kept his eyes on her face.

"Why, of course, sir," she said wholeheartedly. "Where honor is involved there can be no holding back."

"Yes. So I must go. How long it will all take me, I do not know."

"Will you not find difficulties in France at this time?" she asked curiously.

"I doubt it. We Scots are held in friendly favor there,

ever since our Queen Mary was dauphine, though so briefly, and even before. No, no, France has always been a friendly refuge for us. But that is no matter now. I have more to say."

They came to a fork and he moved the horses to the right, down a lane where trees almost met overhead and the sun dappled the dirt. He waited a moment, frowning. "Whether I should say this I do not know, but I must tell you that Lady Sarah, though a grand girl and one who belongs in our Highlands, is not for me. I knew that, though we enjoyed each other's company. There is no reason to go for a great salmon with a light rod and a small trout net."

"But how about trout, then?" she asked mischievously. "You do go for them with a light rod?"

"Ah, yes, the lightest, and my favorite fly, a gray hackle is the best. And I use all the skill the good Lord gave me. And such I would wish to do now but I am prevented. But, when I have discharged my duties in France, may I come to call on you? I have your direction. And then could I persuade you to come north to visit at Castle Athray, with others of course?"

"And if I came would you take me fishing and use a gray hackle?" Mischief lighted her face and brought a lilt to her voice.

"I'll be using my gray hackle from the moment I return to these shores," he said so solemnly she dropped her eyes. "I am happy with you, and though I am not a patient man I can now wait." She felt a curious unevenness in her breath as he stopped.

She thought she heard hoofbeats behind them but they faded. They were at another fork in the lane and she was glad for an excuse to look around, change the subject, dispel what had arisen between them.

"But where are we, sir? There have been so many lanes..."

"A farsighted Scot plans for the future," he told her lightly. "I have a map from Apthorp. This right lane, and some others, will take us back. There is more to say. My home is not like Sir Alec's, but we can improve it..."

They started again, hoofbeats came toward them, and Lord Falkner came around a corner and drew up in astonishment. "Miss Kelway, Sir Angus! How fortunate I am."

Chris wished that her anger could send sparks that would singe his hair. How dare this man interrupt them here and now? Sir Angus had a faint line between his brows for a moment, but answered courteously, "A splendid morning for a ride, is it not, sir?"

"Indeed. I could not resist it...But how fortunate I found you, for these lanes are most confusing and you might have wandered for hours." Only pleasure and solicitude were in his voice.

"We do not need guidance, sir," Chris said swiftly, "for Sir Angus has a map."

"Wise man, but then Apthorp might have made a mistake, for he does not know these lands, perhaps. We move to the right here." He turned his horse and fell in beside Chris, and began to talk genially of the countryside, which he knew though it was not his own, and discussed the Highlands, where he had visited, and drew out Sir Angus, and kept up a steady flow until they rounded another curve and came to the gates of Bouton Abbas. At the front steps he nodded to Chris, shook hands warmly with Sir Angus, repeating his invitation to stop with him when in London, and trotted off around the house toward the stables.

With an ease that was impressive Chris was lifted down from the saddle to face a very serious Scot. "Perhaps he came to guard you," he said slowly, "but there was no need, you know."

"Of course not," she said in low-voiced fury. "He is an interfering obnoxious man."

"My thoughts." His face lightened. "But our time is gone. I am deeply grateful to you, Miss Kelway, for this hour. I will cherish the memory, you laughing in the sun." He nodded once. "And may I say 'Au revoir' and not 'good-bye'? It is my hope I will see you in three or four months. That hope will sustain me." He picked up one hand and kissed it for a long moment, and bowed, took Theta's reins, and strode toward his waiting mount. He looked back once, and she waved, and then he was gone. She went slowly up the steps to the parterre.

The front door opened and Lord Falkner strode through, took her elbow, and marched her from the door to the end of the windows. "And now, my girl, will you tell me what you mean by jaunting off alone in the early morning with a mad Scot?"

"He wished to see me again." The glow was still with her. "It was romantic of him—but you wouldn't understand that, for you have no softer feelings." She jerked her arm away and swung the skirts of her habit around so she could face him. "And he is not mad," she added with sudden fury.

"You say that because he made an offer," and he was very nearly as angry as she was. "After seeing you twice! That's madness. And don't quote Shakespeare at me."

"He did not make an offer." Rage was still with her. "And you are horrid and interfering."

"If not an offer as near as could be. If ever I saw it on a girl's face, a pleased glow no less, it was on yours. And he looked so serious it could be nothing else."

"It is none of your business whatever . . ."

He opened his mouth, closed it, and drew deep breath as his eyes flashed. "It is my business when a guest of my friend is so carried away by a little attention she behaves like a wanton." He was glaring at her as she knew she was at him.

"Wanton! You forget yourself..." and in her fury she raised her right hand that held her crop.

Her wrist was caught, held. "If you try to strike me I will put you over my knee and use that crop on you." His voice grated harshly. "Put it down."

She resisted and implacably her arm was brought down to waist level. "You should have managed better, Miss Kelway, kept your secret rendezvous less conspicuous."

"Managed...secret...You are odious and insulting..." Again anger moved her arm and the grip tightened, then the arm was flung aside so strongly she had to move a foot to keep her balance. That he should speak to her thus! "Your arrogance, your impudence are beyond belief," she threw at him, stammering a little. "You, a thief, to speak so to me!"

"Thief? You dare..."

"Of course I dare, when you insult me. I've refrained long enough...You stole, yes, stole, two of my gold figures."

"What..." His eyes still blazed with fury.

"Only you knew where they were...the crocodile and the snake..."

"But you know why..."

"I can only assume it was for some low foray to the gaming hells of Alexandria," she answered, pushing back some hair that had strayed. "I have tried to forget, forgive, but you said they were mine and you *stole* them." Her voice was still shaking.

"It is you who are arrogant beyond belief...I'll have no more of this..." He whirled, strode to one of the long windows of the saloon, and flung it open. "You had best go to your room, Miss Kelway, and quickly, lest someone else see you."

When she did not move he came back, seized her arm, and took her by a force she could not resist to the sill. "Go," he ordered, "or I'll not be responsible..."

"It is you who are mad," she gasped at the furious face beside her. Wrenching her arm away she ran through the window and up to her own room.

Chapter Twelve

At dinner Lady Lethbridge listened amusedly while Audrey elaborated on the beneficial effects to one's health to be derived from a country visit with its soothing airs and simple way of life that enabled one to recoup one's strength. "And I was so happy to see, dear Aunt, how well dear Christina and dear Jim suited," she ended earnestly. "They were quite inseparable."

"Oh, come now." Chris pretended to bridle. "You are drawing too long a bow, dear Audrey, though I confess we do find each other entertaining. But I was not reduced to just one gallant for the weekend."

"It looked that way to me," Audrey contradicted a little pettishly, "though there was some man in some strange costume who did pay you what might be considered undue attention. And of course others..."

At that moment a large bouquet of roses was delivered to Audrey from Lord Ashburn. "He says the sun has returned to London skies now I am back," she giggled. "Isn't he *silly*!" The other two refrained from comment.

The next afternoon as Chris sat in the library push-

ing her thoughts of the weekend to the back of her
mind by reading, a note was brought to her. Putting
aside her book, she looked at the very black hand-
writing and found it somehow ominous. Her breath
caught as she read the signature, and stopped as she
read the note.

"My dear Miss Kelway,
  As you know, I have a great interest in *objets d'art*
from Egypt, and particularly in gold figurines. When
I saw your collection I felt I must possess it. I am sadly
aware that you would not sell it to me, so I have contrived otherwise. Your dear father has been brought
with me to the so-called Rose Cottage. Here he will
remain, in not too great discomfort, I trust, to be exchanged for your Egyptian gold. There is no use bringing a group to rush the cottage, no one could find him,
or might not find him with saving celerity. If you come
yourself, however, with one friend, this evening, we
will be able to make the exchange. Otherwise I will be
forced to move him to some distance to wait while you
make up your mind. Anytime after eight will be entirely convenient. Believe me, Miss Kelway, your most
obedient servant.   Ashburn.
  I am sure you appreciate that complete secrecy, except for that friend, is essential for the safety of Lord
Ingram."

The note dropped to Christina's lap. This was incredible, here in civilized London. She picked up the sheet
of heavy paper and read it again. There was no doubt
about the message covered in polite language. Of
course she would go. With a friend. What friend? Obviously a man was needed. She dropped the note again
to lie white on her green morning dress. She looked at
the bookshelves. Three faces passed across her mind
in front of the books. Sir Alec, experienced and kind;
Jim, stalwart and also kind; and the one who was not
always kind but was strong and experienced and who

had once, no twice, said that he stood ready to be of service to her father at any time. She shook her head. Lord Falkner was the one man she could not ask a favor. But then, this was not a favor; it was a matter of her father's life. If she went alone Ashburn could perfectly well take her figurines and laugh and carry away her father and then make some other demand. She needed someone who could protect her father.

But it was only yesterday morning Falkner had insulted her and they had raged at each other. He would not be forgetting that. And he had once already come to the assistance of Lord Ingram. That she had achieved by, yes, blackmail, and an appeal to his honor. Perhaps she could appeal to that honor, the obligation he owed her father, again. And, she nodded at the fireplace, she did have a bribe... She must reach him quickly. A note? The footman might dawdle on the way, not impress the butler with the urgency. Falkner's house was nearby on Blandford Street. Too short a distance to take a hackney. Besides that would mean getting Rose, instructing the footman, making some sort of bustle. The only thing to do was to walk there herself. It was too early, and too uncertain a day, for anyone to be already departed for afternoon calls. Yes, she nodded again, and hurried to her room.

There was a side door from a side passage she and Audrey had used once to avoid a gathering of guests at the front steps. The door led to an alley and then to Gloucester Street. She noticed only two errand boys and a nursemaid with a carriage as she sped along. He must be home, he *must*. The butler started to protest that his lordship was occupied and did not receive young women alone anyway but she walked past him and ordered him in her most imperious voice to carry her name to his lordship and conduct her to the small saloon. She would have liked to survey this house, but instead ignored it, colors and all, and went up the stairs with dignity and into the first door on the right, hoping it was indeed the small saloon. Fortunately it seemed to be and she just had time to take two breaths and decide the apricot color was unfortunate when Lord Falkner rushed into the room.

"Miss Kelway! What are you doing here? Where is your abigail? Peters announced you as a young lady alone..."

"And indeed I am, sir. It seemed missish beyond belief not to walk the short distance to your house when I have to see you."

"I'll send one of the footmen to escort you home now," and he turned toward the bellpull.

"Don't you dare to pull that. I'll go when I'm ready." Realizing that was not the best approach toward asking a favor, she amended, "That is, when we have finished. I came to consult you and ask you something."

He halted, swung around, looked at her searchingly, blue eyes wide for a moment. "Then I fear the worst, Miss Kelway. I recollect the last time you consulted me..."

"I recollect *all* our encounters, sir, and have determined I must ignore them." She waved one hand as though dismissing a swarm of bees that were intruding. "Here, sir, do me the favor of reading this." She thought that struck the right conciliatory note and walked over and handed him the letter she had been clutching. "May I sit down?" she ended sweetly.

He indicated a small armchair, stalked to another himself, still reading, sat down and crossed his legs, and looked at her gravely. "This is, well, inconceivable."

He was saying what she had felt, and she sighed. "My thought, sir, when I read it. But I am convinced Lord Ashburn means what he says."

"No doubt..." He was frowning at the window. "If I mistake not, you wish me to be the friend to accompany you. That, Miss Kelway, I feel I must decline. Lord Ashburn holds himself my friend. It would be excessively awkward to confront him on such a mission. And perhaps the situation is not such as would appear at first glance. You should take some other friend."

"No." She spoke as emphatically as she could and leaned forward, clenching her hands. "I have thought. I do not trust that man. Unless I had someone strong with me he could take my figurines and never give up my father."

"Oh, now." Some sunlight from the window made his hair look more yellow than customary. "That is difficult to believe..."

"You are too charitable. He is unscrupulous. You have not forgotten what he tried to do to my father. I need someone as strong as he is."

The wide mouth lifted a little at the corners. "You flatter me," he murmured and looked again at the paper. "But I cannot see my way to involving myself again..."

"You have promised, twice, my lord, to do anything possible for Lord Ingram. This is a matter of his very life, it is evident. I must remind you of those promises. And..." She looked down, her breath a little short, and opened her reticule. "I have brought you a—a gift that may help persuade you." She jumped up and, not wanting to give herself any time to hesitate, went and put on the long hand resting on his lap the rather worn paper from Boulak.

He glanced down, raised his head, and flashed a wide look at her. "The...what you called the marriage license?" he asked incredulously.

She nodded, a little forlornly, and went back to her chair. "Yes. You said you had plans for the future. The very existence of this might conceivably have made them difficult to—to carry out." She put up her head to look at him squarely. "It is yours, so you may destroy it as you wish."

He carefully smoothed out the small paper on his knee and then the letter. "The other time when you asked my aid you blackmailed me. This time you are bribing me?" He looked at her thoughtfully.

"Of course not. It is, as I said, a gift." She meant to put a little hauteur into her voice, but forgot it. "Oh, my lord, it is for my father. You *will* help me?"

"How could I not, in view of your gift?" he said lightly and rose. "It is this evening you are summoned. When shall I call for you? How will you explain your absence?"

"There is a small concert tonight. I will plead fatigue, a touch of migraine. They will leave about eight-thirty."

"Then I will come at nine, and bring my traveling coach, for it will be more comfortable for your father when we return."

She jumped up again. "Yes. Oh, thank you. But do you think my father is all right?"

"I am sure so," his voice reassuring. "He may have been drugged to hold him there, but do not let that worry you, such wears off, you know." His brows drew together. "I do not understand Ashburn in all this. But we'll get your father out, do not worry. It is a pity you must lose your pretties in the process."

"I don't mind that, for Father. I must own, sir, that I am greatly relieved by your acquiescence to my plan." She moved toward the door, satisfied her last words had a proper stately ring.

"How could I fail but acquiesce..." She was sure there was amusement in his voice. He handed her the letter and put the license in his coat pocket. "Wait. I will send for a footman to go with you."

"I don't want a footman," and she continued to walk until a hand caught her arm.

"You will have a footman and if you don't behave properly you will have two *and* my butler to make the procession imposing. Now behave yourself and wait. I will tell Ben to walk behind you." It was obviously useless to argue, and she could not annoy him further, so she stalked back to the side door on the alley, very conscious of a bewildered footman behind her.

At first there seemed nothing to say in the dark coach. Two men were on the box and Chris wondered if that would be considered a violation of the order for one friend, but decided not to mention it. She had slid into the far corner, clutching the blue knitting bag, and tried not to think. Earlier she had taken time to say good-by to the figures, setting them out on the floor to touch and admire. They seemed to grow more enchanting each time she looked at them. The cat stared back at her enigmatically, the owl wisely, the donkey brightly, the jackal inquiringly. Of course she recalled the missing alligator and snake, but put that mystery away, this was not the time to ponder that.

A hand reached out and removed the bag and placed it beside her on the seat. "They will all be quite as safe here," Falkner said softly. "And why not take off that bonnet, fetching as it is, for we have a ride before us and you will not wish to put your head against the squabs with a feather tickling your cheek. We'll put it on top of the gold. I am glad to see you are not fatigued by the country visit."

"No, but I could easily feign at dinner a languid air that was quite convincing," she said slowly. "I could not refrain from thinking . . . is it possible Lord Ashburn is doing this to us out of revenge for his...his setback at the Society?"

"Possibly." His voice was calm and matter-of-fact. "In fact, that may be part of the cause. But I believe it is the gold he is truly after. We will no doubt learn some, if not all, soon. Now, tell me, has the amiable Mr. Purvis been to call?"

"Yesterday afternoon, to inquire, of course, about our health. And he admired Lord Ashburn's extravagant bouquet extravagantly, and Audrey could not tell if he was in earnest and that piqued her."

"As he did when he sat beside you, no doubt. I should have asked him his college at Oxford, though I am sure I did not know him. I may be a little older. Did he tell you about the climbing club at the House, Christ Church, you know?"

"No." The idea caught her attention. "Climbing? I have heard that is the most beautiful college. I hope to see it one day."

"It is and you will. The climbing was an expedition, all done in the best form, you see, proper boots, insignia, though no Alpine stocks were allowed. Done at night, of course, but with a full moon and a prize for the first to make it around every pinnacle of the roof of the church—cathedral, that is. There were spotters who preferred not to climb, to check our progress, and a banquet at the end. It went like this..." The easy voice went on to tell of the exploit and she began to laugh and almost forgot her errand. His reminiscences flowed, and she was caught by surprise when the coach suddenly drew to a halt.

Rose Cottage looked as pretty as its name. Lights behind the red curtains in the four sets of mullioned windows gave an air of cozy good cheer. "How deceiving," Chris gasped angrily as Kirby handed her down from the coach. She stalked up the flag walk and halted. The oak door was dark, ominous in the sparse light from a hanging lantern. Now she was here she was frightened. She had to face an evil man, bring out her father safely. She felt herself begin to choke. The blue bag was being slid into her left hand. Kirby. He was here, how could she have forgotten. She put out her right hand and it was caught and held warmly and dropped. Behind her she heard the coach move and then steps. For a moment she clutched the cloth of the bag, she would show no uncertainty or fear—then loosened her hold and stepped forward.

"Delay just a moment before you enter," Kirby was saying softly. "Then try to see whoever opens the door goes in front of you."

She nodded. He lifted the lantern from its hook and used the brass knocker with his other hand. Quickly the door was flung wide by a burly man in country clothes. "Miss Kelway?" he inquired civilly.

"Yes, and friend," she replied, not moving. She could glimpse the steep stairs behind him, light from the right, on the left the kitchen, where Lord Ashburn was moving back. "Your master is in the kitchen," she said with a suddenly acquired cool clarity. "Take me to him."

The man stepped back and awkwardly took the lantern Kirby handed him.

"Very well. Bring them in here, Henry," Ashburn called.

Chris waited. The man stepped through the door ahead of her, dousing the lantern as he went. The kitchen, low and beamed as she remembered, was lighted by candles on the mantel above the fireplace at the left end of the room and two lamps on the trestle table that stretched below the high front windows and in front of a bench. Lord Ashburn, in a casual coat of deep green, was standing with his back to the rear windows. She moved into the room and nodded toward him.

He bowed, slightly. "Miss Kelway. How good of you to come so promptly. Your father will be pleased. You have a friend with you, I trust? And I saw a coach. So well prepared!" he mocked.

There were steps in the hall and a sound of two hard thumps and "Blast!" Kirby stood in the doorway rubbing the top of his head.

Lord Ashburn looked intensely surprised. "Kirby!"

"The friend I brought," Chris said nonchalantly. She looked back. "What happened, my lord?"

"Damned low beam over the doorway." He was still rubbing the top of his head. "Ducked, but not far enough. Hit it twice."

"One of the penalties of height," explained Lord Ashburn, pleased. "You should look where you go."

"So right, but you should warn guests."

"May we sit?" Without waiting for permission Chris went to the bench that faced across the table, across the room to the armchair near which Lord Ashburn was standing. On her left the tiny fire glowed redly. Four candles in double holders stood on the mantelpiece above it, two surprisingly large lamps rose at either end of the table. Shadows filled the back corners of the room. "It is damp," she said with a faint note of accusation. "Could the fire be rebuilt?" Kirby slid onto the bench beside her, still rubbing his head.

"Henry, wood." Ashburn gestured to the standing man, who crossed to a woodbox on the far wall and brought back kindling and two logs. "You were not expected so early."

Christina drew the bag from her lap and put it on the table. "Where is my father?"

The black eyes glittered at the bag. "The gold? Good. I will see it."

"You have," she returned. "I see my father first."

"You have so little trust! Very well, Henry, assist Lord Ingram to descend to us."

As Henry departed Kirby put his hands flat on the table as if to rise. "May I help?"

"No need, no need, I assure you," the smooth voice purred. "His lordship may be a trifle confused, but that will wear off. He has suffered no hurt."

Labored steps were descending the stairs in the hall. The three sat silent, Kirby holding his head in his hands, until Henry appeared, half carrying Lord Ingram. He was without neckcloth, his jacket and shirt were wrinkled, his eyes half closed, his head dropping forward. Ashburn rose and pushed a small armchair to a place at the inner wall halfway between his chair and the table. Henry lowered the drooping figure into it and stood back.

Chris pushed her way around the table. "Father," she cried as she reached him and put her hand on his.

The heavy eyelids came up. "Christina," he mumbled, but with evident pleasure. "Ashburn said you would join the party later. Sorry, sleepy, must have had too much wine." The face was blurred, uncertain, but it tried to smile. "I'll doze until you wish to leave." The gray head dropped forward again. As Chris withdrew her hand she noticed raw red marks around the wrist. Obviously he had been tied up, but he did not seem to have been injured. That Ashburn should dare to treat her father so! She damped down her indignation, walked back to the end of the table, stretched, and drew the blue bag to her, and pushing the lamp a little back, began to lay out the gold figurines. Elbows on the table, forehead on crossed hands, Kirby sat unmoving. Ashburn rose from his chair and began to walk across the floor.

"It is still cold," Chris said suddenly, put back a

figure, and rubbed her arms. "That fire can do better."
She went over to the wide hearth with the odd hump at one side and plucked from beside it a long iron poker and began to stir the kindling beneath the two logs.

"No," Kirby exclaimed loudly. "You'll be getting them all. You don't have to steal one, Ashburn."

Chris whirled. The poker fell, scattering ashes on hearth and floor. Ashburn's hand was half raised, holding the owl figure. He put it back on the table. "I was examining it to see if it is the same I once saw on another table," he said with surprising mildness. "I may see the others?"

She returned, placed the last two figures beside the others, and noticed the glowing ashes in front of the hearth. She couldn't watch this man examining her treasures. She turned to the fireplace and dragging a broom from a dark angle, brought out a pile of gray ash with it. Sweeping the fiery sparks back where they belonged she reached to do the same for the gray ashes and saw a glint of gold.

The broom clattering unheeded, she dropped to one knee, sought in the feathery pile, and brought out a delicate gold arm holding a broken baton. "Oh." She rushed to the table. "This lay in your ashes," she cried and set it down. It was larger in scale than her figures. The broken end at the top of the arm showed the gold was solid.

Ashburn moved away from the table. The fire, improved, gave a crack as some more kindling caught and flared high and bright, casting its light on his face. She heard Kirby make a strangled sound, but her eyes were on the ruthless features halfway across the room. "What is it?" she demanded.

"I do not need to tell you," the dark voice said calmly. "But yes, it must have fallen off the shovel when the last batch was melted and lain unnoticed all this time. It will go in with yours."

"In? Melted?" Horrified, unbelieving, Chris sat down abruptly on the end of the bench. "You will—destroy these?" Her hand waved toward the row.

"Merely put them to more practical use, Miss Kelway." He smiled, complacently, the black eyes glittering again. "It will be no concern of yours."

"But it is now," she said hotly. "What do you mean?"

"Emotional," he sighed, "like all females. If you insist, this gold, high grade as you see, will be melted into small ingots in that furnace at the side of the chimney. There is little market for gold figures among collectors, at an adequately high price that is. But gold ingots, ah, they bring the highest of prices in the City, best of all in Amsterdam. So your animals there will be put to good use."

She could not believe what he said. "You will melt *them?*" she pointed. "Why?"

"To enable me to live as I wish." He turned impatient. "Once I had another hoard, larger. It sustained me admirably for quite a while. It is in a worthy cause," he added lightly. "I have future plans."

Anguished, she burst out, "How can you? They are so beautiful."

He shrugged. "They are far more beautiful to me as ingots, however small, I assure you."

"I'll not let you have them," she wailed and put out a hand.

"But I have them, and also your father, Miss Kelway. You are in no position to bargain. Henry, stand by his lordship."

The bag was twisting in her hands. She couldn't bear to think of the cat, the owl melted. She looked away, and saw her father. Of course she would have to bear it.

184

Ashburn looked at her. "You're a fetching piece when you are in a temper," he observed thoughtfully. "I hadn't appreciated—you, your father, your gold, the combination is well nigh irresistible."

"No," and it came out as a groan from Kirby's shaking head.

"Get you gone now, man, and don't interfere where you're not wanted." Ashburn backed away toward his armchair and the shelf behind it. "I'm taking charge of Miss Kelway and her gold."

Kirby gave a long, audible sigh, shook his head again, and rose to step back over the bench. "This time you've lost, Ashburn. We are all leaving. Cowan," he called over his shoulder.

As the footman came through the doorway Ashburn twisted sideways, reached up, and a pistol was in his hand as he faced around. "Henry, point your gun at Miss Kelway. We have you, Kirby."

"No," Lord Falkner said yet again. "Cowan has Henry in his sights. We could all fire at once. In such close quarters no one could miss. Undoubtedly we would leave only Lord Ingram and Cowan alive. I admit your targets are more valuable than ours. But I am reluctant to die by a bullet from you, Ashburn." He was speaking a little slowly, eyes and hands were steady. He looked suddenly a little worn, the hollows of his cheeks more pronounced, which made cheekbones, jawline stand out as she had not seen since the days of Sidi. That was it, he looked a little as Sidi had, but at the same time at ease, competent, in command.

"So you had to have help," Ashburn began abruptly, a sneer lifting one corner of the thin mouth as the fire gave a sudden spurt of light. "Miss Kelway did not keep her part of the bargain to bring just a friend."

"It was no bargain on my part," she began angrily.

"You hardly expected either of us to drive a coach,

185

which would obviously be needed out here," Kirby pointed out gently.

Ashburn turned and looked with hatred at Chris. "It is your doing that this has come to naught...I thought you would bring some female to sustain you in the interview."

"You do not know her," Kirby laughed, for a moment his face alight. "She has, as usual, managed quite well. We are going to leave now, Ashburn, the three of us, with the gold. Cowan, give the signal for Paul to come in."

Pistol unwaveringly pointed at Henry, the footman reached behind him and pounded on the door. It seemed within seconds another man, stocky and red-faced, was in the room. "Paul, take the gentleman in the armchair there and put him in the coach. He is drugged and may be heavy. Ignore that pistol, it will not be pointed at you."

"Very good, sir." The coachman walked at the edge of the room, elaborately avoiding interfering in the line of fire, stood in front of Lord Ingram a moment, then reached forward, lifted and put him over one brawny shoulder, and retreated.

"We are at a stalemate," observed Kirby, "and no trust between us. It's not very heroic, is it? Chris, gather up your animals in that bag and come around behind me and go out to the coach. Henry, I see you are now thinking that I present a target for two guns, but do not forget Cowan beside me."

"Stalemate for the moment only," Ashburn said loudly. "Tricked, cheated, I've been. But I'll soon be even with all of you."

"Yes?" Chris heard the reply and paused at the door. "I wonder how. Particularly as I am at last remembering—many things—more clearly all the time."

"You'll be saying it was that knock you got on the

186

head just now," Ashburn snarled. "I've long thought you remembered anyway and were waiting your time."

"You suspect everyone is as deceiving as you are. No, I quite genuinely forgot, a great deal, including the gold you stole from me."

"You haven't an iota of proof," Ashburn sneered.

"Quite true . . . Cowan, shoot the pistol from Henry's hand."

As two shots exploded in the low room Chris ran down the walk. The coach was waiting, the coachman beside the open door. Kirby brushed past her and peered within. "Chris, climb in over your father's legs and get in the far corner. I'll sit here and support him. Cowan, Paul, up on the box and back to town. Though," with some satisfaction, "I don't think either of them will be wishful of following us until their hands recover from having their pistols shot away."

In two minutes the coach was moving briskly. Chris watched as Kirby lifted her father a little and drew him so that he was supported by a strong shoulder and an arm around his back. "Oh, good, you are a better cushion for him than I would be."

"Assuredly. With your permission, I will take him to my own house and keep him overnight, perhaps an extra day or so. We can care for him better than would be possible at his hotel and there is no need to alarm the Lethbridges."

"Yes, do keep him. He will be so much more comfortable with you. Thank you for the thought. But . . ." she remembered something ominous, "what did that evil man mean when he said he would be even with us? Will he pursue my father again? Or—or try for that gold he said he needs?"

"I'll keep your father until he is himself. Cowan is excellent when one is under the weather and whatever Lord Ingram was fed to put him in this state can be

187

soon counteracted, for I am convinced it is not poison but some disorienting potion."

She gave a gasp. "I had not thought of poison. Oh, I am relieved you do not believe it is that..."

"No. But what Ashburn is plotting I have no idea. If I had I would try to guard against it."

"He was blaming me for foiling his plans... And he was furious that you were beginning to remember."

"As I am beginning, and will more, I believe, when this headache leaves me. Which," and he let out a great breath, "will be most welcome. I have not known, you see, what I might have been, have done, during the period I can't remember, and I dared not look to the future for fear something might come to light, be discovered that would entangle me in, well, something base, abhorrent."

"Even in a place as far away as Egypt?" she asked curiously.

"Even that. I dared not risk—anything. But now, when I can sort it all out, I can follow my desires."

Briefly she wondered if Lady Ottilie figured in them and hoped not quite violently. This surprised her and she murmured something about wishing him all success and put her head back against the squabs, as there seemed nothing more to say. For a while she lived again through the scene in the cottage kitchen, blotting out the houses and fields revealed by a half-moon. So much seemed impossible, now. She had been so sensible to bring Kirby, she told herself complacently. Without him, why, anything might have happened. Beside her her father stirred, there was a soothing murmur, and she found she was drifting into a doze.

When the coach stopped Cowan helped her down from the far side. Then Kirby was holding her arm firmly and guiding her up the steps. "We are but back from Lady Finley's," he instructed her rapidly. "I came by. Your head was better. I persuaded you to accompany me. It was a concert, you remember, with an Italian who screeched, just in case anyone inquires. I will come tomorrow."

At the door she stopped and held out her hand. "Again, I thank you. And I wish," quite seriously, "to congratulate you on how well you managed everything." For the benefit of the footman, she smiled widely and went through the door.

As she put away her gold figures in the chest she was reminded that two were missing. She shook her head. How could a man who had done so much for her father have stolen from her?

Chapter Thirteen

Her sleep had been so sound that when Christina awoke she was surprised that she felt so happy. In a flash, however, she remembered. Her father had been rescued and by Kirby, who had been all kindness and consideration, and had managed it all so effectively. Vengefully she deplored that Lord Ashburn would escape with his evil intentions a secret, as he had before. But Kirby had rescued her gold figures from the melting oven, which was another element, though slight, in her happiness. And he had told her not to concern herself with Ashburn's threat, and that he would come today. She would ask him how much, what he was remembering of that lost time. Perhaps it would be everything, even to that evening in Boulak. But even if that quick ceremony had been lost, and if it had it must have been from some other reason, perhaps unwillingness to acknowledge what had happened, it would make no difference. He must have destroyed that paper as soon as she left the house—no man would wish to be reminded of a marriage forced upon him. She would not mention it, of course, but perhaps courtesy would bring him to say something, and laugh, and say they could both forget that, as of course she could. No wonder the sun was so bright this morning. She wished she could tell him all over again how grateful she was ... even though he had turned her attempt aside. She would take Audrey on a walk, for it was too good a morning to rest indoors.

She listened with more attention than usual to Audrey's description of a small rout and a new flirt Jim Purvis had had the impudence to escort. This last subject was introduced with a sidelong glance at Chris, who looked brightly interested.

Tea had been brought before Lord Falkner joined them. Jim Purvis was already making himself agreeable to both girls with what seemed like practiced ease. Lord Falkner took a chair between Lady Lethbridge and Chris and turned to the lady. "Lord Ingram had charged me to get word to Lord Lethbridge, ma'am, that he will be unable to meet him after dinner this evening as they had agreed."

"Oh?" Lady Lethbridge was pouring him a cup. "No indisposition, I trust?"

"In its own way, ma'am, but temporary only." There was an amused note in his voice. "We encountered each other rather late last night. Neither of us had had luck at cards so we went to try together at roulette and to everyone's surprise won a little. That, of course, we had to celebrate."

"I trust you were not foxed," she said with an understanding twinkle.

"Certainly not, ma'am. At the most a little above ourselves. That is to be expected. As my home was nearer than his hotel we decided it would be delightful if he spent the night with me. This morning he decided he was so comfortably cared for that he would accept my invitation to spend another night or two with me."

Since it was evident that every word would reach

Chris she turned and nodded. "How fortunate my father is to have such a good friend, my lord. His social life may have been more wearing than he has realized. Tell him not to come for a visit here until he is quite recovered."

As he bowed and promised Lord Ashburn appeared in the doorway. Chris knew her jaw dropped and shut it quickly with what seemed to her a loud snap. The impudence! He was the customary smooth man of the world, greeted all, and took a chair next to Audrey. Lord Falkner rose in a minute, bent to murmur something in Lady Lethbridge's ear which made her laugh, and bowed himself away. Since Ashburn was monopolizing Audrey Jim turned to Chris and she began to rally him about his new friend. He did not lower his voice as he spoke enthusiastically of Miss Celia Mountliard, and Chris saw Audrey become a little absentminded in her converse with Ashburn as she tried to listen. Lady Lethbridge leaned back in her chair and smiled at them all.

When, the next afternoon, Chris and Audrey saw Mr. Purvis driving in his curricle with a dashing redhaired beauty beside him who could be no other than Miss Mountliard, it was no wonder that there had been nothing but praise for the new beauty. Chris was quite content to be beside Sir Alec, but Audrey turned fussy and petulant toward Mr. Bowman until both turned silent. Chris wanted to shake her. Sir Alec's twinkle showed he understood the situation and was amused, for which she was grateful.

It was a different Audrey who tugged Chris into her room after tea the next day. The girl had been driving with Lord Ashburn and on her return had sent word she had a headache and would retire until dinner. She had been waiting for Chris, for she had flung open her door and pounced, shut the door, and settled them both on the bed.

Audrey's cheeks were a little flushed and her curls in disarray. She looked perkily pleased with herself and proud, but there was fright in her eyes, too. "I could not wait to tell you," she began in a rush and stopped, pulled out a handkerchief, and began to roll and unroll it. Her breath came out with a gasp. "I have just refused an offer from Lord Ashburn. And, and he did not like it at all."

Chris refrained from giving a cheer. "Tell me about it," she suggested calmly.

"That's what I'm doing." Audrey stopped again. "We went driving and we came to a place under a big tree that was quite secluded. He stopped the horses and moved nearer to me and took both my hands and said he could not live any longer without me and I must marry him at once or he would shoot us both." Her eyes widened at that and a frightened look took over for a moment.

"What did you do?"

She tossed her head at the thought. "I laughed at him. Wasn't that famous? I did not know I would. It just came out. He sounded so *silly*. But for a moment he looked so mad I thought he meant it."

"Of course he didn't," Chris said matter-of-factly.

"I'm not sure." Audrey was not to be deprived of a little of the drama of the situation. "But he asked why. He said I had given every evidence of enjoying his company. So I told him I did, that he had been most agreeable, but that he had been too *easy*, too obvious about his plans. And I told him I was not a country miss to be carried away by attentions and then, I sort of rose above myself and became quite the lady and told him he should have approached my father or at the least Lord Lethbridge to ask permission to pay court to me and I preferred to have things done in the proper fashion as a true gentleman would. He got mad at that too, and looked so murderous I could have fainted if I had tried, but then I did not see why he should be mad so I told him to drive me home and not to speak to me again."

"What next?"

"Why, nothing. He bowed and drove me back and it was indeed dull not to talk but as I had said not to I couldn't." She leaned forward, pleading. "Oh, Chris, tell me I did right. I truly do not wish to tell anyone else, though they will see he no longer favors me with his attentions. But I do not truly care about that, for though he can be very entertaining I have come to feel he is not *nice*. I wish I had thought to tell him that, too," she said sadly.

"I'm sure you said enough." Chris could not hold back a giggle at the picture of the two silent on the front seat of the curricle. "Yes, my dear, I do think you did exactly right. He would not make you a—a good husband."

Audrey's flower face crumpled. "Now I haven't a fascinating man who wants to marry me," she gulped. "I don't think *I* want to, I just want some unusual man to want to. It makes a girl feel so much better. The others who say they do are so dull."

"Of course," Chris agreed and for one forlorn moment knew how Audrey felt, then decided to set Lady Lethbridge to finding some new men for Audrey, which would surely comfort her.

The following night, an hour before the Lethbridges were due to leave for Lady Comblay's ball, the butler announced that the back axle of the large coach was broken. That seemed impossible, but when Lord Lethbridge investigated himself he had to acknowledge it was broken indeed, but in a fashion he had never encountered before. Interesting but not of assistance, his lady pointed out with asperity. They would have to divide the party and use the two small traveling coaches. The girls assured her that since it was only some five streets away they did not in the least object to going that distance by themselves.

The ball was small, for two pretty daughters, and so plentifully supplied with young men that various rules about dances had to be relaxed and it turned into a laughing game for the young people, who thoroughly appreciated the change. And most of the gentlemen were hitherto unknown, for Lord Comblay was with the Admiralty, which added to the high spirits of all.

It was well after midnight when the coach carrying Chris and Audrey pulled away from Grosvenor Square and made as if to follow the Lethbridge coach in front. It did, slowly, for three streets, and then, out of sight of the first coach, turned a corner and another and headed in a different direction entirely. The girls did not notice.

Since Lord Ingram had insisted on removing himself to his hotel Lord Falkner had dined alone and then dropped in on two affairs looking for two pretty girls, and not finding them—he had not been invited to Lady Comblay's—had ended up at a club where he encountered Mr. Purvis, also at loose ends. They tried their skill at roulette and found it vanished and finally sauntered back for a nightcap at Lord Falkner's. Both were preoccupied. With the glasses half empty Mr. Purvis finally burst out, "What is it, sir? You are concerned . . ."

Falkner smiled ruefully. "I admit it—though so are you—I cannot divine about what or how something I dread will occur. And you?"

"It must be evident that it is Audrey Cadwell who is my chief concern. I cannot remain indefinitely in

London. But I cannot leave her to be snatched by someone like that Ashburn. I admit, sir, I do not know which way to turn."

"Understandably. And . . ."

The footman knocked and entered. "Symes is here, sir, with some word." He was pushed aside by a small dark man in a black suit. "It's happened, sir. We watched for the young ladies, didn't guard their coach, followed it when it left a ball, but it turned off. Only then saw not same two men on the box. Last saw Haley going after a hack to follow."

Falkner's fist slammed on the table beside his chair. "I should have had three men watching, not two." He rose. "Purvis? We'll stop by your place for your arms. Symes, order my phaeton, send me Cowan, he's coming with us, you are to go on an errand, a long one. Any clue as to direction?"

"Seemed to be north, sir, toward Islington."

"That blasted cottage. We'll try it, though I doubt its use now, too obvious. I'll be ready in five minutes, Purvis, and will explain what has happened as we go."

The other watcher, Haley, was not come up with until at the cottage, where he and the hackney were conspicuously waiting. "They were here, sir, but only stopped for a man to pick up a message. He called out to the cook as he left they were for the north road. It was the same coach, I know, sir, and I could hear the two young ladies talking a little, angry-like."

"They can't be going to Gretna Green," Jim Purvis exclaimed, looking down from his seat beside Falkner.

Haley shook his head. "Only place, sir, unless there's a friend's house along the way."

Obtaining a description of the coach and men, Falkner set the phaeton moving briskly. No one would pay attention to a coach passing the busy Angel, but four miles farther an ostler had noticed it because the horses were tired. Six miles farther the coach had not been seen at a sprawling inn. Falkner jumped down, motioned to Jim, tossed the reins to Cowan, and strolled into the bar and ordered four pints of the best, one for his man outside and one for the landlord, and leaned on the counter. "Looking for a friend," he confided in a drunken sputter, "forgotten name. Big house. Between here and Is—Is—Islington."

Obligingly the landlord brought out three names Falkner dismissed, then said, "There is Lord Wilby's place, always someone there."

"That's it," cried Falkner, smashing down his hand on the counter. "Wilby."

"You don't look like a guest of his, sir," the landlord objected hesitantly. "We see some of them here. The womenfolk too. That house don't have so good a name roundabouts, sir."

"Got to see Wilby, get directions for finding the place," Falkner insisted, threw a coin on the counter, and jerked Purvis away from his pint.

"He's a bad 'un," Falkner said as he turned his pair. "Don't know him but by reputation. Hellfire Club type. Kind of friend Ashburn would have. Most other men too respectable to know him."

In the half moonlight Lord Wilby's home merely looked blandly secret, all the windows covered by colorless draperies, no smoke from the chimney pots, dull light only in one string of windows on the first floor. Falkner halted the phaeton in a shadow on the unkept sward beside a rutted driveway. "I'm sure I'm right," he said slowly, "but in case I'm not no need to make a spectacle of ourselves. I'm taking this right-hand drive and trusting it will bring us to the stables." He half turned his head. "We don't want to shoot, Cowan, but we will if there's a need."

The drive did circle the building at a small distance

and came at it on the side and through an archway that led to the stable yard. A black coach with drooping, untended horses stood at one side. Falkner backed the phaeton until it stood on the sod outside the wall, tied the horses loosely to a post, dropped his greatcoat on the seat, and strode through the entrance. There was subdued bustle from the far end of the stable and subdued light from what appeared the kitchen wing. There a door ajar showed a scullery, a corridor, a large kitchen, and light and voices beyond. Through another door, in what looked like the housekeeper's parlor, three men were visible around a table which held one empty bottle of whiskey and two full ones. Falkner drew back, pulled out a pistol, and took it by the barrel. Purvis nodded and followed suit. "You take the one on the left," whispered Falkner, "I'll manage the other two. Then Cowan can tie them up."

It went as easily as he said; the men were half foxed and bewildered and quickly made secure. A door opened showed them into the house, a corridor, followed by a soft light and then a brighter. At Cowan's whisper, "All tight, sir," they crept down the hall. "Guard them, Cowan," Falkner ordered and moved on and up the stairs.

On the far side of another hall lay a block of light, and with the light came Audrey's voice loud and clear. "I've already said I am not going to elope with you or anyone. It is outrageous to kidnap us this way. You are to take us both home immediately."

That was followed by a laugh and a snicker. Falkner put a hand on Jim's arm.

"This is the most unpleasant and unseemly jest, Lord Ashburn. But it is played. You have mystified us, caused some uncertainty. Now we will go to the coach. And," Chris added spiritedly, "if you are going to say the men will not drive us I assure you Audrey and I are capable of driving ourselves."

"Splendid, splendid," said a voice like a bray. "My dear Ashburn, I am in your debt for bringing the girl to me. What pleasure she will furnish."

"Don't let that—that badger touch me," Chris warned. "I'll throw the tea set at him."

"It takes more than a tea set to deter Lord Wilby from his purposes. When he is having his way remember if you had not managed so cleverly about that gold this might never have happened. Audrey, put on your cloak, we'll have to drive to the next inn to change horses."

There came the sound of a crack and a cry of protest from Chris. Falkner leaped through the door. "What are you doing to my wife?" he shouted furiously.

The people in the room froze. Chris, left arm upraised, was beside a table facing a man who held high a small whip. Ashburn was holding Audrey's cloak at her shoulder.

It was Audrey who broke the silence as Jim moved from behind Falkner. "Oh, Jim, save me from this dreadful man," she shrieked.

"Of course, my dear," he gritted. "Ashburn, *en garde,*" and his rapier slid from its sheath as Ashburn dropped the cloak and backed to a clear space.

"The country bumpkin," he sneered as he jerked out his own weapon.

As Falkner took another stride forward Chris dropped her arm, where a red streak was forming, and turned a white, frightened face to him. "Oh, *Kirby,*" she whispered.

"Wilby." Falkner's voice was now icy. "I've heard you were evil. And no one stopped you. Now I will. You have dared touch my wife." Despite his rage he kept his gaze fastened on the thin feral face before him. The man did look like a badger, a receding forehead slanting from a pointed nose, chin running backward, the whole focus on three overlapping, protruding teeth. The effect was strange and obscenely menacing. Falkner drew his rapier. "Over there." He jerked his head. "Where there's room to fight." He stepped sideways, watching as the other man did likewise to a cleared area of the red carpet. From the right came the clash of blade on blade and heavy breathing.

As he stood, waiting for the other man to draw, Wilby suddenly had out his weapon and jumped forward. Only a leap backward and an instantaneous defense saved him. "Chris," he called, "move farther back. I must teach this animal a lesson."

"You can't." The pale eyes gleamed with an exultant malice. "I've heard of you, too, Falkner. I've got your girl. As you die you can think on the pleasures she will bring me." And he sprang forward again.

As the blades slithered against each other and disengaged, Kirby knew that he was out of practice and the man was an expert. Wilby giggled. "Well done," he approved and his rapier feinted, disengaged, and came on again.

After that it was engage, disengage, lunge, feint, retreat, Falkner's whole attention concentrated on the pale eyes. Even when he heard an ejaculation, a heavy fall, a cry from Audrey, he watched. And for one vital second Wilby's eyes flicked across the room. As they did Falkner stretched to his utmost and put the point of his blade through Wilby's right shoulder, knocking down the other's blade as he withdrew his own. The wound was too high to do serious damage but at least it was incapacitating. Wilby, eyes astonished, fell.

Falkner looked to Jim. Somehow, perhaps in disengaging, Ashburn had run him through the left thigh. Audrey, screaming, "You shan't kill him," had flung herself on top of Jim's body. Chris had run, snatched the rapier from his flaccid hand, and was pointing it at Ashburn, gasping, "Leave them alone."

Ignoring her, he swung around and faced Falkner, his eyes flickering to the figure of Wilby on the red carpet. "I'll be blasted," he said loudly. "Never thought any man could take him."

"His own fault, I must confess. He looked to you," Kirby acknowledged. "He's not much hurt, unfortunately."

"Neither is your friend. So, what do you say? You've saved Miss Kelway from the unpleasant attentions of Wilby. Miss Cadwell's childhood friend is somewhat incapacitated and no use to anyone. And here you and I stand. What do you say? I'll take the beauty and her fortune north and you take the other lady south. You and I have nothing against each other."

"You are forgetting more than I thought even you could," Kirby said matter-of-factly, resting his reddened tip on the floor. "But, first . . . Chris, Audrey, pull Jim over to that couch by the door. He's too heavy, you can't lift him. Put a cushion under his head and wet some napkins in that carafe of wine and mop at the wound. It's not deep, do not agitate yourselves about it. He will recover quickly." He had not taken his eyes from Ashburn. "If you have any desire to do aught for your friend," he said politely, "I promise I will not interfere or take advantage."

Ashburn snorted. "Not a friend. I was using him as a convenience and he has undone me. Let him die."

"Gladly. Now you were saying . . ." Falkner shook his head. "I don't think your idea is feasible, too many will object. But, before we get to that, there is something that has puzzled me." He was speaking as casually as though of the weather. "Why did you wish to
201

have me killed there in Egypt? We had had no quarrel. As far as I knew our relationship was friendly."

Ashburn brought the tip of his own rapier down to the floor and watched as the two girls seized Jim by the arms and pulled him across the floor to a sofa. He looked back to Falkner. "I had no thought of having you killed, believe me; you were my meal ticket and passage home, until you found that gold. How did that happen, by the way? Come, we are not pressed for time. Tell me now. There was no—er—chance to learn."

"No." Kirby looked at him thoughtfully. "You didn't give me any, did you? I know now and must conclude it was that knock I took on my head at the cottage that brought it all back. I found the gold by accident. I hired a boat to take me across the Nile, to what they call the Valley of the Kings, you remember, and I just wandered along the cliffs, my pockets pulled out to show they were empty. I turned by chance up a narrow space between cliffs and in a moment heard a cry. Inside a remote cleft two men were beating an old man. I shouted and knocked one man down and as I beat him and told him never to touch the old man again, the other ran away. Of course he couldn't understand my words, but eventually he took my meaning and I let him go and went to the old man."

A glance showed him that Chris had left Audrey to bathing Jim's brow and crept up to a chair behind the table to listen. "There was a tomb behind him," he resumed. "He pointed; I went in and found one of those water jugs and brought it to him. I did have some money hidden, so I went and got a chicken, some of that flat bread, and some fruit and another jug of water and took it back to him and we ate together."

Though his eyes did not move from Ashburn, his voice grew dreamy. "Then all of a sudden it was dark and I knew I couldn't get back to the river. He did too

202

for he gestured that his tomb was mine, so to speak. He did know that I was a foreigner. And he made some gesture about lying down that seemed to me he was showing he'd be dying soon. After a while he got up and lit a torch and motioned me to come after him. We went farther back in the tomb, very rough-cut it was, and at one corner was a pile of rocks. He motioned to me to move them, and I did, and there was a passage and we went in and down and then to another and came on a room that wasn't empty like those we'd passed. It was filled, quite neatly, with furniture, some full size, some miniature, some inlaid with gold, arms, small boats, and gold statues of different sizes. He made a sweeping gesture as if to say it was all mine. He left me, and I was afraid he'd never come back, but he did, with some wrappings from a mummy, you can tell by the cloth, you know. He'd made them into a sack, and he began to pile in gold figurines. We did up the bundle, it was quite large, you remember, and I followed him out and up to his tomb and put the rocks back where they'd been. Then we slept."

"Just the luck of a fool," Ashburn said angrily. "How'd you get the bundle across to our camp?"

"My ancient did that. Kept me there all day. Went out and got some stalwart man to come just before sundown, guide me out to the river by a roundabout valley, and deliver me to a man in a felucca. And then there I was, in the chief's tent, showing the gold to you and laughing. The cream of the jest is, Ashburn, that I was going to take you back there so we could share in the hoard of gold and treasures. If you had given me time to tell my adventure you would have held back whatever hand it was that struck me."

"Damnation," Ashburn said slowly. "It was the laughing that set my mind. It was so damned unfair— you had everything already, and I had lost my last cent. I had to have that gold. But I couldn't get it if you were still around. I had no desire to kill you myself, but someone else could and I'd never really know. You were hungry. I went to get some food for you and while you were eating talked to some big wig called a sherif. Our interpreter was a knave and a crook. They'd have killed us both, but I told them first the English and French were coming back the next month and would kill all the people along the Nile, wherever, if foreigners were hurt. Guess I made it sound good. But there was that gold. The interpreter said another sherif needed a slave, good at figures, imposts, so many new taxes, new collectors, and no one knowing what was what. Ibn-El-Hahir would pay for such a slave. The life was hard . . . You'd last one year, two at the most, he said. So it was settled, and for right then. I knew if I waited it would cost me more."

"How much were you paid for me?" Kirby asked with interest.

"Twenty Spanish dollars, enough to take me to Alexandria, I thought. But the old fox cheated me, gave me Spanish dollars without the two pillars on one side, and no one would take them. Cost me a figure of a duck to get down the river and a dancer to pay for my passage home, and the interpreter took another. Cost me a pretty penny, you can see. But there was a lot of gold, so I made out very well by the melting. Carried me for nigh two years." The words dropped into a silence. They were compelling and Chris listened appalled. As he spoke of a figure of a duck he had had to pay a thought shot across her mind, something important, and then was gone as she listened. Then Jim groaned and tried to move and Wilby, across the floor, rolled over on his face.

Lord Ashburn, frowning darkly, looked at Audrey sitting beside Jim, at Chris behind the table, at Wilby, and last at Falkner contemplating him gravely. The black eyes narrowed. "I guess we are at a stalemate again. You'll take the young ladies and your impetuous friend and depart. I'll stay and see what I can do for Wilby and leave tomorrow. After all, you have nothing against me now."

"Nothing?" The hitherto calm voice cracked and the face twisted with anger. "Nothing, Ashburn?" There was a moment's pause and when he spoke again his voice and face were under control. "You forget. You deprived me of two years of my life, and left me with such a despairing ignorance of what had happened before I was struck that I could not order my existence. Because of you I wore the leg irons of a slave for a year, worked in the fields under a blazing sun, suffered beatings, constant hunger, a vast bewilderment for months, jeers of the other slaves, then close confinement to create orderly records where none had existed in a language I'd never known, and, when I escaped, exhaustion and thirst that almost finished me. You call that nothing? To cap it all you have caused my friends anguish and distress. Add that to my total and, yes, I hold much against you."

Ashburn had glowered through the recital. "Very pretty," he now mocked. "You have made a case for yourself. But you are here, and recovered in every way. I do not hold myself at fault for what happened to you."

"Even though it was your doing that I so suffered."

The heavy shoulders shrugged. "The turn of a coin." He hesitated. "Do you mean to try to kill me? You won't, you know."

"No, not kill." The voice was still even. "I am going to wound you quite severely so you may learn what it is like to be sick, penniless, without friends or recourse."

"A vain hope. But come, let's settle our score. This

room is made for contests." He gestured with his rapier at the length, the white walls hung with panels of red-and-white-striped taffeta, the chairs and sofas all pushed along the edges of the red carpet. "You have friends here. You guarantee no interference?"

"There will be none."

Before the words were finished Ashburn had raised his rapier and sprung forward to attack. Falkner backed, threw up his own blade, and caught the other's. For a moment, two shining lines of steel crossed above their heads, and they stared at each other. Simultaneously they disengaged and retreated, and Ashburn came on again. He fought fiercely, as though by weight and speed he would overcome his opponent, but met a steady defense. There was ample room, and once again it was press forward, move back, amid the unrelenting sounds of tap, tap, slither, tap, engage, riposte, the rest of the world shut out. But not quite. Falkner heard a sound of slithering on the floor at his left, but he noticed it only in passing. He knew his wrist was tiring. Ashburn was as fresh, as violent as ever, forcing him in the direction of the table. From behind came a sharp cry. Falkner retreated again, and warned by a sudden gleam in Ashburn's eyes, leaped to his right as the man sprang forward, rapier and arm outstretched, and plunged forward with all his strength. Someone shouted and someone groaned and a body fell and Audrey screamed. Blade still raised against an opponent who was no longer before him, Falkner spun to his left.

In spite of the color of the carpet the trail of blood showed that Wilby had dragged himself toward the center of the room pulling his rapier with him, had steadied himself on his elbows, his rapier held point forward in two hands. Ashburn evidently had seen that, had driven Falkner back toward that point and then rushed forward with all his strength to force Falkner either to impale himself from the back or to receive one from the front, and been unable to stop himself when Falkner jumped away. For now he lay, impaled, fallen across Wilby, who gave a groan.

"What's happened?" Jim called querulously. "Falkner, are you all right?"

"Quite," Kirby said over his shoulder in an odd voice. "In fact, we are all quite all right, now." He walked to the table. Taking a napkin to wipe his blade he looked seriously at Chris. "I heard you warn me. Thank you."

"I could think of nothing else to do, seeing that man holding up his sword so firmly." She gave a shudder and stopped. Then, "I so hope that horrid man is dead."

"Can't we go home now?" cried Audrey plaintively. "It must be very late. I am so tired and Jim should have a surgeon."

Kirby thrust his rapier back in the scabbard. "Yes. I'll have you out of this room in a minute." He left it and was back with Cowan and a man in the livery of a footman, who gave one curious glance at the heap on the floor and averted his gaze to allow there was a saloon with wine and cakes waiting at hand that would be more comfortable for the ladies. With Cowan's help Jim was assisted there, a room that showed black and gold when lighted. Falkner and Cowan left for a few minutes and returned to say to no one in particular that both men were alive and the footman would go for a surgeon.

"I'm sure they don't deserve to be," Audrey spoke around some cake, "but perhaps they won't be for long, what do you think, sir?"

"Only a surgeon can predict," he replied with reserve and directed firmly that they were to eat, for even cakes and a little wine would make them feel more the thing. Setting an example, he took a chair and a little cake covered with almonds.

It was Audrey who revived most quickly. "Wasn't Jim just *wonderful*," she breathed happily. "He fought like a tiger and saved me from that dreadful man." Ignoring his deprecatory mumble she turned a radiant face to Falkner. "Oh, and I do thank you, my lord, for coming with him, of course, and helping that man to kill himself, perhaps, though I didn't see quite how he did it. But it was Jim who saved *me*."

Falkner bowed, not looking at Jim, who was muttering something to Audrey. She took another sip of wine and looked under lowered lashes at Chris, who was working on a chocolate cake. "I do hope you won't mind, dear Chris, but I have decided that I do not care for London. The air, you know, so heavy, and you cannot deny that strange things happen. And there are too many people. I have quite made up my mind to return to Somerset immediately. Jim said he had to leave, you remember. I do realize he has a slight *tendre* for you, but he had one for me long before he knew you and I cannot believe it has vanished." There was no doubt in the limpid eyes and the smile she turned on Jim was ravishing, enough to make any man forget a leg wound. "It hasn't, has it?" she demanded with serene assurance.

"No," Jim said heavily, putting one hand over hers that lay on the table.

"So that is all right," she ended complacently and took another bite.

Chris could not resist looking at Falkner and caught his eye and they nodded at each other without expression. It was such a comfort to have a friend whose mind met with yours on occasion. Friend—and memory flooded back. That was not the word he had used when he burst into the room. What did he mean by saying *wife* when she was no such thing? Was it to startle those men, give himself the best of reasons for rescuing her? But since then he had shown it meant nothing to him but a device. She looked at him as he lifted the wineglass. His face was calm, the hollows in his cheeks a little more pronounced than she recalled, perhaps from strain, fatigue, from the last hour, and no wonder. This man was not Sidi, he had an assurance that Sidi had never had. He was not quite Lord Falkner, the impeccable gentleman of the *ton*. This was a business-like, competent man alert on every count. He set down his glass, rose, bowed just a little, and murmured, "Horses," and left them.

Chris had finished another delicious cake while watching Audrey move her chair close to Jim's and rest her head on his shoulder and had reflected how fortunate it was his leg that was hurt, when Falkner returned.

"Miss Cadwell, Purvis," he began briskly, "Cowan will drive you in the coach. It will be slow to Islington, for the beasts are weary, but you can change horses there and go straight to the Lethbridges. Tell them the truth, but no one else. They will find a surgeon for that leg. Any excuse, such as a broken trace, will do to account for the late return. I am taking Miss Kelway in the phaeton." He put Audrey's cloak around her, helped Jim into his coat, put one arm over his shoulders, and assisted him to the door, Audrey twittering behind. There he turned toward Chris. "Would you be good enough to wait here a few minutes, Miss Kelway? I will return quickly."

She nodded but they were gone. Thoughtfully she took another cake. Ashburn had revealed something to her. She had to tell Falkner, and she was uncertain how to go about it. Leaning her head on one hand she began to draw lines on the tablecloth, but they were no help and before she found the answer Falkner was in the room with her own cloak over his arm. "This is hardly enough for a drive in a phaeton at this time of night," he said, "but upstairs Cowan found some blankets for the coach and I held out one for you. You are not too weary to walk to the stables, I trust," he asked a little anxiously.

"I am not weary at all, sir," she told him vigorously and took his arm. At the phaeton the footman was waiting. Yes, he would send for a surgeon to see to Lord Wilby and he would take care of everything, he promised, and he would release the two bound men when that had been accomplished.

"And you know no names." Falkner was evidently repeating an injunction, his hand bringing something from his pocket.

"Quite right, sir," the man answered stolidly, "and there were no ladies here this evening."

"Good." He bent to tuck the blanket a little more firmly around Chris's feet. "Then we are off." And he started the horses toward the driveway.

Chapter Fourteen

A spreading glow in the east had driven away the stars, bringing trees and hedges and cottages out of the blackness. It was quiet except for the horses trotting, and peaceful, so welcome after the last hours. It had all been appalling, from the moment they noticed the coach was going through strange streets and found the door was tightly fastened. She had been fearful, she acknowledged, then, and on the drive, but somehow reassured when they stopped for only a moment at that cottage. Perhaps it was only a joke, a prank, she told Audrey, which had been found comforting. But when they had come to the strange house, and been forced to descend and then enter and mount the stairs under threat of being carried if they could not walk, she had been apprehensive. Then that hateful red and white room and the two men, pleased and mocking.

"I was truly frightened." To her surprise she said it out loud.

The head above her, outlined against the sky, turned to her. "And quite rightly." The approval made her feel better.

"Yes. I think they expected us to go into high hysterics and to enjoy that. I was determined not to, but I was ashamed of myself for feeling such terror, and quite at a loss to know how I should manage."

"In the circumstances it would have been exceedingly difficult, but I am sure," and now there was a touch of laughter in the grave voice, "you would have managed—something."

"I cannot believe that, and oh, I was so glad to see you. I had discarded all hope we would be found." She must evade the matter of his entrance, for that word he had used was pressing her and she must not use it or remind him of what undoubtedly had been used to startle. "I am grateful beyond words for your arrival sir."

"Then don't bother your head trying to find some," he advised, still with amusement. "I am happy to be of service to you."

She was still in that room, facing that horrible man. "He wanted to use his whip, you know. No, my arm does not hurt, it just stings, for he said it was a light taste of what would come." She found herself shuddering again. "I was about to pick up a chair to fend him off, but I could not have lasted long."

"Pray stop thinking on it all," he said softly. "It upsets—us both. I should have killed him but I am glad I did not, either of them, for the consequences would have been awkward and interfering. But it is all over. I beg you to put it out of your mind."

"I'll try," she said with a meekness that surprised her. "It *is* over, but when you spoke, toward the end, to that appalling man, you told how you had found the gold, your own gold. So you must have recovered what happened before that point was reached. What were you doing? What *did* happen?"

He laughed a little. "A sad anticlimax, after all my anguish and despair. Nothing had happened. I had not been guilty of theft or murder or any of those things I might have done if I had been truly out of my mind from illness or drugs. We were in Cairo. We hired a boat to take us up the Nile, smaller than the dahabieh of your father, slower. We did a little shooting, for sport, bet on which kite would leave a palm first, that sort of thing, never collected our bets, went to admire the temples. It was at Thebes that Ashburn, acting as if it was a great joke, told me he had not a feather to fly with, not even a sparrow's, to get him home. It did seem something of a joke, and I told him that did not matter, that I could get us both home and he could repay me then. He said he did not know how he could, but it was still a joke, on me for having gone along with his idea of the trip. And then I found my own gold. It was too much for him. He prefers quick action, as you have seen, and—he acted almost instantly, before I could tell him my plan for him. I confess I feel quite young and giddy since I learned all that, foolish as it may sound. I am convinced it was those two knocks on my head, one when I did not bow far enough and then when I straightened, combined with seeing Ashburn across from me, firelight on his face, gold between us, that brought back to me that last evening in Thebes."

"But how satisfactory you have discovered all." Chris found she was feeling light-headed herself. "It may seem a setdown to a gentleman to find he has not done violent things when he feared he might, but it is very reassuring, also, you have to admit. I am glad for you. And to have it all settled, and on such a lovely night." She hugged herself. "The moon is rising, see, and it will be even more beautiful."

"Assuredly. We are coming to the Angel, where we must change horses. I will drive into the stable yard and leave you briefly while I arrange for fresh cattle. Do you mind?"

"Of course not," she answered dreamily, for a slate roof had suddenly shone like silver and taken her mind to the gleam of roofs in London, and then to those of Wiltshire. Perhaps Audrey was right and the country was preferable to London. Well, she would be leaving soon enough herself, and she felt a pang, for that meant leaving behind people, too, and she would miss them.

They came down a closed and shuttered street to the large, still-lighted inn, and the wheels rattled over cobblestones. "I won't be long," Kirby promised as he left her. She had hardly time to contemplate regretfully certain people she would be leaving behind in London before the horses were being removed from the traces and two others backed into place, and, after inspecting the harnessing, Kirby was in beside her and they were moving more rapidly out of town.

Chris brought her mind back to her obligation. She might as well get it over with. The blanket had warmed her, but for her duty she pushed it back and straightened. They were out of the village now and into a softly glowing night with fields and trees shining back at the sky. Somewhere a cow mooed and then a fox barked twice. A wood brought dusk suddenly and she felt now was a good chance to begin, for he could not discern her face.

"I have," she began and stopped. It was more difficult than she had expected. "I," she began firmly again, "have a deep apology to make to you, sir, and I do not quite know how to do it. Nor can I account for my grievous mistake." She felt he looked down at her.

"Go right ahead," he said cordially. "We all make mistakes."

"But this ... I should have known better. I regret that I ever called you a thief. I did not realize until tonight that it was to procure money for our own passage to England that you took those two gold figurines
214

and that without your so doing my father and I might have had great, great difficulties. I hope you will forgive me." Her voice trailed away.

"You infuriated me, you know, with that accusation. "I thought it must be obvious to you. You seemed ungrateful and stupid, which appalled me. I could not understand. I felt lacerated."

"But why did you not tell me?" she wailed.

"Of course I could not ask for gratitude you did not have to give! Never."

"I am so *sorry* I was so—so unjust. Can you ever forgive me? And the things I said to you?"

"I have, long since. And you? Can you forgive my—insults?"

She gave a gurgle. "Oh, yes, though I was astounded and furious. I even forgave your saying I was managing. But then, you were so good to Father. I could forgive anyone who is that. But still, I should not so have misjudged your character for even a fleeting moment."

"I can see how it came about, and quite natural."

"But," and she frowned at a passing hedgerow, "there is one thing I did not, do not understand. When I first spoke to you, reminded you of the days on the Nile, you said you had no idea what I was talking about. You gave me a horrid setdown so I did not dare remind you later. But why?"

She peered at him and could see he was frowning in turn. "My denial came to me instantly. I did recognize you, though you looked so different, your hair cut, a formal dress . . . But always I moved with that cloud at the back of my mind, those lost months. I might have committed murder, theft, robbery, anything is possible in Cairo, and at any time someone might recognize me, accuse me, and I would have no defense. And it might be true. I had prepared myself, in case I should encounter you by chance. I could not involve you until I knew. And even when we did speak of our time together there was still that blank space. That made me hold my tongue about—many things."

"Yes," she agreed slowly. "I can understand. And if I could be so wrong about you, why, others might be also. But I am glad to know, for that was of deep concern to me. I was so glad to find you, and then to be rebuffed, you see, was very downcasting . . . and I felt I had lost a friend."

"Don't. You had not, but I dared not acknowledge you in any way. Your thought is distressing."

Now he seemed in an answering mood there were other mysteries to uncover. "You could have asked me, told me, that you wished to use two of the gold animals on our behalf."

"There was no time. I could not speak in front of your father, for he did not know of them. If I was to get the money for your passage I must act in haste."

"But how did you?"

He was deprecating and a little proud. "By gambling. On the dahabieh I played nights with the crew, learned much of their games, which were simple compared to some of ours. I asked the reis for a goldsmith and found him and paid him to cut the gold into pieces which could be used, for quite high stakes I must add, and where were the gambling rooms that would admit me. I used to play in London, long ago; it seemed quite natural. I went to three, to avoid too much notice, and did well."

"Did you win *all* the passage money?" That was impressive.

"And more too, which I kept as my commission, I told myself. I stayed to investigate in Cairo, I had to have money for that, for my passage, for England when I returned. I went back to Cairo, found some better clothes, gambled some more with even greater success.

216

Then I set out to find and meet the few Englishmen who had been in Cairo when Ashburn said he had left me ill nearly to death with a physician. There were only a handful and they had stayed in the city, whereas I *knew* it had been at Thebes that I was struck. None had heard of an ailing fellow countryman. Also I called on some of the physicians, but none had had a dying foreigner left in their charge."

She remembered her father saying that the young man walking away from the ship would do very well alone. "What happened next?"

"I won some more money and took passage on a Turkish ship bound for Marseilles. There I became almost a gentleman again and made my way to Antwerp and thence to Dover."

"How enterprising of you." There was no other word. "One thing more, how did you learn your title, home, family?"

He was enjoying recounting his adventures. "That came to me suddenly as we entered Dover. I was home. I *knew* where I was, and who I was and where my home was. All that came, but not those crucial memories of how and why I was hit on the head and deposited with the sherif, and what had gone on just before. That was what kept me from speaking to you of many things. My honor would not allow me to until I *knew*."

Men seldom talked of their honor, but it did seem sometimes to get in the way of common sense. As it had with this man. So much trouble could have been spared her if he had come out right away...She wouldn't have cared about the lost time. But at last...she sighed happily.

He was going on... "In London, when I could meet my friends, I pursued my search. By the way, I did have my hair cut entirely off in Cairo, and I did buy a wig. I wished you were there to pass judgment. Since

217

Ashburn, as you know, told me flatly he had left me in Cairo, I tried to discover any Englishmen, agents, merchants, explorers here who might have been in that city. I found only a few, and no clues at all to what had happened to me. So I was at a standstill. Then you appeared. I knew I *had* to learn of that time, and was in despair when I could not. And there you were. Several times I almost confessed all, but could not. You should have only a whole man, not one with a black cloud in a portion of his memory. I had to bury my joy at seeing you, my wish to tell you everything, explain everything, and settle everything. I only knew as I suffered from those deprivations that I was fortunate that I had learned to suppress all I could not, did not wish to show. I had to be so careful. I hope never to go through such anguish again as I felt every time I was with you."

"I would not have cared," she flashed at him. "You should have known that."

"But your father would have. I came near to telling him when he repaid the money, but I found I could not."

"I'm not so sure. He liked you, the two of you, and he would have approved highly of your honorable conduct."

"Have you any more questions, my dear?"

The last words distracted her. Why use them? "No," she whispered, afraid he would take them back. "Thank you for answering..."

"So, good, then all is clear between us. And high time, too, and just in time."

"Time for what?" The blanket around her was a cozy cocoon, making her drowsy.

"If you will move nearer and put your head on my arm," he advised, "you will be more comfortable."

Forgetting he had not answered her question, she
218

edged along the seat until her shoulder encountered a firm arm which she found she could lean against with ease. She did, then shamelessly she realized and ignored the thought, snuggled closer until her cheek was on his sleeve, and drifted away. A halt and a call brought her sleepily upright. Beyond the horses' ears she could see open gates and trees. Beside her Kirby was leaning down to speak to someone she could not see and then straightening and setting the horses forward.

She threw back the blanket and blinked at passing trees and then up at the man beside her. "What are you doing?" she asked with a calm that made her proud, for undoubtedly he had lost his way if not his mind. "Where are we?" If he was truly lost that should jolt him.

"I am glad you are awake," he said, with an odd note of excitement in his voice. "This drive was made longer than was needed, to add consequence, you see, by the third lord, but we will arrive at the proper time, when all is ready. You feel better after your nap, I trust? You seemed to sleep quietly."

"I did, sir." She threw the blanket back farther and looked around, but there were only large trees and their shadows. "This is *not* London," she announced. "It is not even one of the parks. Have you lost your mind after your efforts tonight?"

"My efforts, as you kindly term them, have brought me something for which I have longed and could not achieve all these past months. In a moment you and I will arrive at Fallends." The strange note was still in his voice. The phaeton rounded a rising curve and the trees were left behind. "And there it is."

He did not need to point. They were curving again to come before a house that stood facing the moonlight. It rose from above two terraces. It was long, three stories high, and made of brick, from which the moon had taken all color. The windows were long and between two small round towers, flattened against the center of the house, a wide door stood open. Somewhere water was falling. Looking for that homely sound she found, at the ends of the terraces, the glittering pillars of four fountains. The whole scene was serene and assured.

"It's lovely," Chris gasped. "But . . . ?"

"No lovelier than its new mistress. Come, my darling."

Kirby was out of his seat and around at her side, holding up his hands. She rose, caught one foot in the blanket, and stumbled and fell into his arms. "Well done." He chuckled a little and she felt a kiss on one temple as he set her on her feet. "Come," he said again, and put her hand inside his arm and walked her up the wide shallow steps, across the first terrace, up more steps and another terrace to the door. She tried once to pull her hand away, but it was held firmly against his side. And all the time he was talking rapidly. "It's called Fallends, no one knows why but so it has been always. The first baron built it, thanks to piracy and Queen Elizabeth, and the others have had the good sense to leave it alone, except that my grandfather knocked the small rooms into larger ones that are quite comfortable. In fact it is a comfortable house at all times. I so much hope you will like it."

They were before the open door. He turned and picked her up in his arms, and laughed, this time with a note of what could only be triumph, and carried her over the sill and through the entranceway into a hall not very well lighted and set her on her feet. "Can you come up the stairs?" he asked. "Or would you prefer I carry you?"

The dimness after the blaze of moonlight blinded her for a moment and she clung to one of his arms, but dropped it. It had been so quick. But this was all wrong. She turned back toward the door. "It is very handsome, sir," she gasped. "But now you must take me home." As she said that her heart sank, for it would be hours before that could be reached. Something must have disordered his mind.

"No, no," and the infuriating man was laughing again. "You must be famished. There is a supper waiting on the first floor, in the saloon. Here." He seized her hand and led her quickly up a flight of stairs into a room well lighted by candles that vied with the moonlight streaming from the windows, and toward a table spread with glasses and dishes. He nodded at it approvingly, and removed her cloak. "You haven't guessed, love?"

This was the outside of enough. She whirled toward him. "Guessed what? What do you mean by bringing me here, and alone? You are no better than that awful Ashburn."

He looked at her so tenderly she felt her heart turn over. "Oh my love, you don't understand yet. To what better place than my own home could I bring my wife?"

She put out a hand and found a straight chair to grasp. "But I'm not your wife..." she began rather faintly. "You have no right."

"No right?" One eyebrow went up. He was facing the window and she could see him clearly, face and eyes alight with amusement and much more. "No right? When I hold a marriage license?"

"You don't. You must have destroyed it instantly."

"Never. I have cherished it—I can show you it, anytime, and another one too I've been waiting most impatiently to use." His look turned a little quizzical. "Don't tell me you object."

"Of course I object. You are bemused out of all reason. We are not married ... You have never shown the slightest interest in me in—in that way."

"How could I until I knew about that lost time? It was when I woke that morning after we had rescued your father from Ashburn's cottage that everything was clear. My first instinct was to rush to you, tell you I was a man freed from any doubts, proclaim to you and the world we were married. But some reason came to me. I had prepared for much of this already, since it was only a matter of time, but I knew I needed to make more arrangements. I knew, too, I must hurry. Ashburn I could not trust. And there was Sir Alec. He was poised on the knife edge of offering ..."

"That I do not believe."

"Your rendezvous with the mad Scot almost brought Alec to the point, within ames ace. If it hadn't been that he learned of it just as he was about to say farewell to his departing guests and you were among the first to go I am sure he would have made an offer right then."

"Oh, no, I cannot believe that."

"You don't have to, now. No doubt he was as mad with jealousy as I was. I should have thought of that ride myself, and if I had there would have been no one to interfere with me."

"You were abominable, and you know it."

"Oh, yes, but with such good results—he never had enough time alone with you to press his case." He paused for a moment while she drew ragged breath. "I did not realize Ashburn would act so quickly, that very day, though I should have, have stayed by you, protected you other than just having men posted to watch and warn me. So when I learned you and Audrey had been driven away, I knew this was the moment, that I could compass everything I had so long wished—his downfall—and of vastly greater importance, of course, bringing you here. You told me I was not romantic, you remember. I determined to show you I was not cold, that I am deep in love. What could be more romantic than this..." He stretched his arms wide. "To bring my wife, by moonlight, to my home?"

"But you couldn't have known it would be like this, have managed everything," she faltered.

"But I did indeed manage everything I could, beforehand, and this night, when I heard what had happened to you, I knew I could bring about what I so much desired." He moved nearer. "And I have," he exulted and took her in his arms and kissed her lightly.

"No. You—cannot." Her arms had moved up to go around his neck quite without thought, but as she spoke she realized what was happening and instead pushed him hard away from her and ran to the door. She was flying down the stairs, trying to think. The phaeton was there below the terraces, she could get to that and drive away and at the first village find the road to London. She picked up her skirts so she could run faster and was through the entrance and on the terrace when she heard steps behind her. She was down to the second terrace and falling water was filling her ears when her shoulders were seized and she was twirled around and held so tightly she could hardly breathe.

"Chris, my darling, don't run. I'll just have to catch you again," he was saying, and kissing her so hard she gasped when he lifted his head.

"You know you love me," and his voice was unsteady. "I've loved you since that night you found me at Clio's tomb."

Remembering, she leaned back against his arms. The moonlight, the black palms, the shining river, and the white sand. That moonlight there was harsh and stark. What was around her now was softer, more pleasing. She raised her head and looked at him, eyes wide. This was Sidi, the man she had found, but he was more than Sidi, he was Kirby Derwent, Lord Falkner, a man who loved her and would care for her and whom she loved and had loved for so long. Eyes wide, he was looking at her intently.

"Oh, Kirby," she began, then rushed on, "I must have, too, but didn't know it and then wouldn't let myself. I do love you."

"Then I must tell you, before I let myself kiss you again, that we are going to be married in the church here in three days. I have a special license and I'm sending notes to your father and the Lethbridges to come down for just one night. Purvis and Audrey too, of course. We're to be married in the morning, so they can start back after luncheon and leave us alone, here, and I hope you approve."

She began to laugh. "Oh, I do. You've managed beautifully."

"And I'm going to manage you, and cherish you and love you for the rest of our lives." His head came down and she lost her laughter as she answered his kiss.